A Novel

THE FACE
OF GOD

JEFF MCKENZIE

CHAPTER 1

A FACE IN THE DESERT

"God created mankind in his own image, in the image of God he created them; male and female" Genesis 1:27 NIV

Wind and sand are billowing and blowing all around. A large white wall and a dome are visible in the distance through the blowing dust. The desert is hot and the sun is almost blinding between the gusting wind and blowing sand. A flash of white and another blast of wind! The wind is blowing so hard, stinging David's eyes that he cannot focus on the white object off in the distance. He tries to raise his arm to shield his eyes, but the effort is too great. The brightness prevents him from locking onto anything specific as he sweeps his gaze from left to right. In between the gusts, he can just make out a brick wall off in the distance to his right side. To his left there is only a hazy emptiness. He looks up at the sun. It is an orange globe unshaken by the blowing wind and sand. It appears to be racing across the sky, but David knows it is an illusion caused by the maelstrom of blowing sand. David tries to force his mind to concentrate on this moment, "Why am I here? What am I doing in this strange place? I don't recognize anything around me and I can't remember how I got here."

But it is difficult, and his mind and concentration keep being pulled back to the white object. Between gusts he is able to discern the white object is a woman, and she is waving. No, he realizes she isn't simply waving. She is beckoning him to come to her with pleading gestures. There isn't any haste in her actions, Her arms are undulating, almost begging him to approach. Her long white robes are flowing in the breeze. They seem out of sync because they are billowing like a flag on a breezy day, not whipping frantically in the same wind that is David's constant onslaught. It is surreal because the windstorm only increases with another blast to his face. She is there beckoning, but it seems like she isn't part of the same storm around him. She continues to gesture for him to come to her. David looks away feeling the sting on his cheeks from the sand. He tries to walk in her direction, but his feet feel as though they are held down by heavy lead weights. Each stride is met with increased resistance, and his frustration only increases with each attempted step. He cries out, but is met with a muted silence. The harder he struggles, the more mired he becomes in the sand unable to make any forward progress. His feet won't move and he lashes out at the storm which only disorients him more. Suddenly, he feels another presence off in the distance. A somewhat muted voice, then clearer; "David!" He becomes aware of someone speaking his name. He looks over and the person starts to move closer and closer until the face is right in front of David. He recognizes Kathleen, his wife. She is trying to pull him away, but he desperately wants to reach the woman in white, and he tries to pull away, "No, I have to get to that woman! She holds the answers!"

❖

"David, WAKE UP!" Kathleen shakes David trying to disrupt him from his dream. She has been steadily increasing her shaking in an attempt to awaken David, but he is almost trancelike in his dream and delirium-like state. Finally, with one violent shake David's eyes open and stare at Kathleen almost unrecognizing his own wife.

Kathleen says, "David, I've been shaking you for a while now! I didn't think you were ever going to wake up! What in the world were you dreaming about?"

David rubs his eyes and wills himself to shake the dream from his head. He looks at the clock next to the bed. It reads 4:48am. He sits up and puts his feet on the floor. "I don't know. It was so strange and unnerving. I still remember it vividly, but can't explain what it was all about. The dream didn't feel like it was anything from this world!"

Kathleen looks at him and wants to ask something, but says, "I have a pretty full day ahead. I'm going to try and get some more sleep. Are you sure you're okay?"

David shakes his head again, and deep down the answer to her "are you okay?" question lies a much deeper discussion for another time because no, he is decidedly not okay. Instead he replies, "Yeah, I'm fine. It was just a very weird dream. I think I'll get up, make some coffee and put some finishing touches on my sermon for this week. I know I've said this before, and I do love pastoring a large church, but having Saturday evening service along with three Sunday services definitely puts a strain my time, and my weeks feel more and more compressed. I finish up on Sunday afternoon, and Saturday comes right back around before I know it."

"I get that! Plus, all your meetings with staff and congregation members coupled with commitments to the community, you definitely have your hands full," Kathleen responds, "the old Dolly Parton song *Working 9 to 5* sounds like a dream job sometimes!"

David kisses Kathleen on the forehead and says, "I wish!" She rolls over, and settles to go back to sleep. As he slips on his slippers to head downstairs. He stops, looks at his feet, lifts them up and down and says to himself, "Strange! Not so heavy now, are you?"

David stands and reaches for his bathrobe. He carefully strides out of the bedroom and softly closes the door behind him. Remnants from the dream still dance around his head as he tries to find the meaning around the strangeness. He had such a strong urge to go to where the woman was waving. David isn't a mystic in his beliefs by any stretch, after all he is the senior pastor at a large Christian church, but he knows this dream is somehow speaking to his heart, if he could just understand how to unravel its meaning. The dream would be slow to fade today, as it was on previous days. How many times has he experienced some version of this dream? This has to be the 8th time in as many nights. He should have said something to Kathleen about the details of the dream the very first time. Each time the dream has intensified and revealed additional details from previous dreams. Now, it just feels like he is keeping something from her which bothers him. At the same time, he doesn't want to worry her about something that will probably turn out to be nothing. Even though holding out on Kathleen is bothersome, the dream itself bothers David to the core because each time it happens, he knows it holds the portent of ominous things to come. David heads downstairs and starts a pot of coffee. He pulls out a sketchpad and pencil.

At the age of seven David got an Etch-A-Sketch™ from his uncle and was fascinated by the art he could create. On his next birthday, his parents got him his 1st sketch pad and pencil set, and he was hooked forever. David took the sketchbook everywhere he went. He started drawing still pictures of everything he could find: animals, statues, fruit, balls, plants, people. It didn't matter what the subject, David wanted to render all of it onto his art pad. Along the way, he got to be very very good. He mastered shading and color matching. He learned he could draw in broad strokes or fine intimate detail. His finished products were high quality works-of-art and he had several framed and on display around the house and at church. He even considered art as a major to potentially follow as a young man, but being the son of a pastor eventually drove him to enroll in seminary and follow a similar path as his father.

David uses his artwork as an outlet to help him escape his busy days and many responsibilities. He can feel the stress and pressures of daily life melt away as his mind begins to focus on a drawing. As he flips through the pages of the 11 by 14-inch sketchbook, he stops momentarily on his current subject, Patricia Erin, his daughter. He promised Patty, he would do a formal sketch and watercolor for her birthday. Before starting the project, he studied several pictures of Patty to get a feel for how he wanted to draw her. Knowing how much she loves animals, he wanted to incorporate an image of her holding something she could cuddle and care for. After a few failed attempts with puppies or kittens, he settled on a picture of Patty holding a dove just as it was about to take flight. The key to the whole picture is how he renders Patty smiling as the bird begins to fly free. He knows he will complete it this week which gives him a sense of satisfaction. He wants to continue on Patty's picture, but feels compelled to work on a different sketch while the dream from this morning is still fresh in his mind. He continues to flip until he reaches a page that brings the dream back into the fullness of his conscience!

The drawing is the desert scene from his dreams, and he begins sketching, trying to add as many additional details from his dream as he can remember. Previously, he didn't remember the dome, so he adds that detail to the page where he had previously sketched only buildings. He adjusts the color of the sun to be orange, but hazier from the blowing sand. His portrayal of the women beckoning him is haunting. Her face is mostly in shadow because he doesn't have the clarity of seeing her eyes, nose, mouth and cheeks. The drawing has as much detail as he can pull from his memory, and it almost chills David as he looks it over and remembers how real it felt only a short while ago. David gets up after a few minutes. He goes to the kitchen and pours himself another cup of coffee. After sitting back down, he closes his eyes and says a small prayer before drinking his coffee. "Lord, thank you for the many blessings you have bestowed on me and my family. Please watch over Patty, Kathleen and our congregation. Give me discernment and clarity in dealing with Your church. Help me navigate these uncertain times with strength, and help me to understand this recurring dream. In Your Son's name I pray. Amen."

After a while, Kathleen awakens and comes downstairs. She walks in while David is drawing, and glances over at him. She heads over to get a cup of coffee. He quickly places the picture under several sheets. Kathleen sees him shuffling the drawing under the other papers. She pours herself a cup of coffee and joins David at the table.

Kathleen thinks about asking about the drawing, but says, "Good morning, sweetheart. What are you drawing? I thought you were going to work on your sermon."

David holds up the sheet on top, "I was just working on this picture of Patty. I promised her I would finish it up for her birthday. What do you think?"

"Oh David, it's beautiful. Has Patty seen it yet?" Kathleen comments. She knows he has discreetly avoided showing her one of his drawings. She pours herself a cup of coffee and sits down across from David.

"No, I told her she couldn't see it until it was finished. I completed the details and then I recently added the watercolors. The colors and the lighting were difficult. It was hard to get the skin tones exactly the way I wanted. The dove's wings were challenging as well. Usually, I'm just a sketch artist with grays and blacks doing all the work. Adding the color was a real challenge, but I think I pulled it off." David adds, "Hopefully she will be pleased with the result. I was going to show her this morning when she wakes up."

Kathleen reaches for the drawing and holds it up, "Of course she will! You've captured her eyes and her smile perfectly! The balance between the light and dark areas is superb! I'll have to think of some projects you can do for me next!" She hands the drawing back to David, "Have you finished up your sermon for tonight? What's the topic going to be?

David replies, "it's done except for some final touches. It centers on the theme that we know Jesus existed, and from the Bible we know His works and the many miracles He performed. But, we don't know what Jesus actually looked like. My sermon will have the best impact if I can get everyone to envision an image of Jesus in their minds. Once the image is implanted, I'll ask everyone to remember that image, and to bring up the image in their minds whenever they are struggling with sin in their lives."

"And how are you going to get your congregation to envision an image of Jesus?"

David smiles and pulls another sheet from his stack of pictures, "With this! I have been working on this for a couple of weeks now. Do you think this will capture my congregation's imaginations?"

Kathleen stares in wonder at the picture before her. She reaches for it and turns it into the light to grasp it fully. David has skillfully added his own flair with traditional clothing from Jesus' time, but the artistry is magnificent. The picture shows Jesus looking downward at His hands. He has a very sad and mournful look. "That's incredible! You never cease to amaze me with your drawings. I can definitely see how this will help people visualize Jesus, but why did you draw Him so sad?"

David thinks about it a moment, and a flood of emotions come to the surface. He is still a bit charged from his dream earlier and working on the other drawing from that experience, so he's not quite ready to discuss all of his feelings. He pushes them back down into the recesses of his mind and says, "It's just the image that came to me. It's strange because when I started, I had no pre-conceived notion of how I wanted to draw Jesus. The image just came into my head, and I couldn't shake it until I had finished with the sketch. I guess I wanted to draw Jesus in a sad way because I'm dealing with the topic of sin. We all sin, but I believe it makes God sad when we sin." David tries to lighten the mood so he smiles and says, "Besides, you know how we artists are a moody and sentimental lot... I thought I would only be able to draw sad clowns, who knew? What's for dinner tonight?"

Kathleen takes David's answer in stride and decides not to press on the other issue, "Chicken and dumplings, oh, and please come straight home tonight. I've invited a couple to dinner who just moved into the neighborhood, Brittany and Dan Landing. They seem very nice, and I thought it would be a thoughtful touch to invite them over, and introduce them to the very distinguished Senior Pastor of The Shepherd's Christian Church! They indicated they were looking for a new place to worship and were very involved in their previous church."

"Kathleen! You know I don't like to make plans right after Saturday service! I never know what may come up," David replies. He realizes he's responded too harshly and softens his tone, "Ok, I'll try. But you know how people demand my time and attention especially after they have been moved to tears by my stirring sermons!"

Kathleen, not one to shy away from her own version of quid pro quo, "well I don't know about that, but I do know you have a talent for driving me crazy! Just be home as soon as you can! I know weekends are tough on your schedule, but it was the only night available for everyone for a couple of weeks. Can you please manage to make it a priority?"

They are both a little more upbeat now, as Patty, their thirteen year old daughter bounces into the room. She stops at each parent and gives them a hug and a peck on the cheek.

"Morning mom, morning dad!" Patty asks, "What's for breakfast?"

Kathleen responds, "Your dad and I are just having coffee. I can fix you eggs if you want, or just pour a bowl of cereal. How did you sleep?"

"I slept great! I would love some scrambled eggs and toast!" she replies. "I'm so happy it's summer vacation! And my special day is right around the corner, hint, hint!"

"I'll get right on that special order. Oh, and by the way, speaking of around the corner, your father has something he wants to show you!"

Patty asks, "Seriously? Oh dad, did you finish it?"

David looks sheepishly at her and asks back, "Finish what? I'm just sitting here drinking my coffee, minding my own business and not understanding anything you are saying. But, I guess that's normal for a father of an around the corner 14 year old daughter!"

Patty goes over to him to poke him in the ribs, but David grabs her and pulls her onto his lap and begins to tickle her until she squeals in surrender.

"I give up, I give up! You're such a tease. My picture, let me I see it! I'm begging you!" Patty says in between gasping for air.

David continues to tease her, "only after you promise to love it and cherish it forever!"

"No promises!" Patty teases back.

David stops the tickling and lifts Patty back on the floor in front of him. He reaches for his sketchpad, pulls the drawing out and shows it to her. Patty looks at it and pulls it close. She exclaims, "Oh dad, I really do love it! It's beautiful. I can't believe you finished it. Oh my goodness, the dove spreading his wings and flying from my hands is brilliant. Is there any special meaning behind that?"

David responds, "you know everything I do has meaning, and I love the fact that you saw it right away. I'm so proud of the young woman you have grown into. I won't say I'm not a tiny bit sad, and miss that precocious little girl that had me wrapped around her finger from the day I brought her home from the hospital. But I see a future so bright and promising for you. I love being your dad and teaching and leading you into that future. I know your wings are sprouting and soon you will be flying on your own. So, as you guessed that is the message within the drawing."

Patty adds, "actually, is it finished? Because I see you haven't signed it at the bottom."

Patty's last comment touches a deep chord within David. Signing a painting was something David was always uncomfortable about. He was the product of a father who was also a preacher and his dad drilled him constantly about the sin of pride and being a humble servant before God. It was hard at times, but he never doubted his talent and treasures came from God. He was a talented artist, but since his talent came from God, he rationalized signing his name at the bottom of his drawings would be an act of pride. "Patty, you've asked me this question before. And no, my stance hasn't changed. My ability to draw this picture is a gift from the Lord, and signing the picture would just be pride on my part. End of discussion!" Changing the subject, David asks, "How are your art classes coming?"

Patty responds, "Let's just say I haven't been blessed with the same gift with drawing as you, but I am enjoying it along with my dance class."

David continues, "Well, keep at it, and the gift will come. I like some of the drawings you've done. You do have a real talent in the making. You just have to stick with it. So, what do you and your mom have planned for today?"

Kathleen steps in to answer David, "I am taking our daughter shopping for her birthday. I figured it was easier to let her pick out something she really liked rather than making two trips, one to buy it and one to return it for something she really wanted!"

"Oh mom, am I really that hard to buy for?" Patty wonders.

David asks, "Do you know what you want?

Patty smiles and says, "My motto is: Life's short, you can never have enough shoes, so buy more shoes!"

David reaches over and grabs Patty and pulls her to his lap and starts tickling her again. "Oh yeah, well my motto is tickle them until they beg for mercy and make them promise to buy fewer shoes!"

Patty wriggles herself free of her dad and shouts, "Never!"

David rolls his eyes in mock exasperation. He loves his relationship with his daughter. She is bright, quick witted and self-confident. She reminds him a lot of himself at that age. He wonders what the future holds for his daughter. He would love for her to find a life working in and around the church, but he doesn't want to interfere too much in her choice. He knows they have laid a good foundation and have balanced her spiritual life with her worldly values.

The three of them sit around the breakfast table and continue to talk and laugh. Kathleen tries to not put too much thought into the awkwardness from earlier, but she knows something is troubling her husband. After they finish breakfast, Kathleen and Patty spend some time getting dressed and then they both kiss David as they leave to go shopping.

David is alone. He places the picture of Patty back in the stack and pulls out the picture drawn from his dreams. He sits staring at the picture. He closes his eyes and leans back. The picture comes back to life in his mind. The same scene with the domed building, the wall with people, and off to the right the buildings with the woman in the white billowing robes waving her arms for him to come to her.

CHAPTER 2

A FACE IN CHURCH

"Now faith is confidence in what we hope for and assurance about what we do not see" Hebrews 11:1 NIV

David's life journey has brought him a long way since seminary school where he dreamed what the future would hold for him. His desire to follow God was founded early in his life being the only son of a preacher in the mid-west. His father was always tough, but fair with his discipline and teaching. He was a pious man and it would fill David with confidence to witness his father's faith and devotion to God. Dad never wavered in his faith and belief, at least outwardly to his family and close friends even when tough economic times hit. They certainly were not wealthy according to world standards, but his parents provided well and never skimped on their love. Since David was an only child, he didn't have to compete with siblings for his parents' affection. David decided early on he wanted the life his father had modeled for him; a life in the church helping people to have a richer and deeper understanding of the love God has for each of us.

Now, as David walks into his church, he is overcome with a wave of emotions. It has been a wonderful mission creating this ministry, and working alongside his friend and mentor, Bill Martin. They met in seminary and discovered early on how each man's talents and gifts complimented one another. Bill was an organizer and an exceptional planner. He didn't make a move without already knowing where his next five steps would land. David was an idea man and related to people in a way that inspired them. He had charisma and self-confidence. The two of them together made an impressive team. Their friendship grew and after seminary they decided to try their hand at church planting. It was a rough go for a couple years, but their small church kept growing, and finally reached a point where they were sustaining themselves and their small staff. They put all their trust into what God was doing in the life of their church and took a large leap of faith by breaking ground on a much larger facility. They asked themselves and their congregation to leave their comfort zones, and to walk with them and to take a "step out in faith." They never looked back. The church grew and people came to hear the word of God. David was the lead pastor and the face of the church. Bill was the executive pastor and planned for the business, staffing and facility needs. They worked well together as a team because their spiritual gifts complemented each other so well.

Despite all their outward success, lately David was troubled and having doubts about his long-term future with his church. Even before his dreams started occurring, David was feeling something was missing in his life and in his ministry. His faith in the path he was following was no longer clear in his mind. He always had a vision for what he wanted to do and the role he wanted to play. He had settled into his role, but now he didn't know if that role really fit him for the long term anymore. And worse, deep down, he didn't know the root of what was causing him to feel this way. He loved to preach his sermons. As much work and consternation they caused him creating them each week, giving the sermons still brought him great jxoy. It was something else altogether causing him to re-think what the future looked like. There were a lot of business strains with the ongoing upkeep of the church. Bill handled the business side of the ministry mostly, but David was still a part of the managing, planning and execution. He loved the people coming to the church, and he had a variety of different levels of contact with them. It wasn't the same as when they were a smaller church and he had a deeper personal relationship with every member, but he still prided himself in knowing all the church's members as much as possible. He read their prayer requests every week and knew most of the struggles they were having. He couldn't put his finger on the exact nature of his anxiety and feelings, but he felt the church should do more to help those in need. As David sat at his desk reflecting on his feelings, he heard some of his staff arriving which made him put aside these thoughts and concentrate on his sermon for this evening. One more review coupled with a couple tweaks, and his sermon was ready. He emailed the sermon to his technical team so they could display the prepared notes and sermon points on the screens. They would do a walk thru of the service to make sure everyone knew their cues for each transition. It was amazing how technology had changed the church. Not only would David reach several thousand people in person over the course of the weekend, but his message was also being viewed online. He hoped this extended reach would have an impact on people's lives near and far.

One of the things that made David such a successful pastor was his approach to delivering his sermons. His sermons always struck a chord with his congregation as he personalized the scripture in a way that made it relevant to people living in a modern complex world. His sincerity also resonated with the people in how he delivered his messages because he practiced what he preached. On top of that, David delivered his sermons with passion. He elicited strong emotions from everyone in the building including himself. Tonight was no different as he delivered this sermon. David stood tall in his pulpit, with one hand holding his Bible in the air, and the other tracking in his notes, "...The Gospel simply means 'the good news' and it is a special journey for each and every person as they begin to understand what this good news means for them and their daily life. Many people initially reject the invitation because they feel they don't deserve God's grace and forgiveness. They carry a heavy burden of shame and regret from the sins of their past. How could God love a person who sins so easily? And if we are all honest with ourselves, know we will sin again and again regardless of our attempts to live without sin in our lives. Guilt prevents people from trusting other people, and so they miss out knowing the one person who only wants to love them guilt-free. The one person who holds them blameless and sinless. Instead, they must somehow earn God's love by performing good deeds and being a good person. By the way, there is nothing wrong with good deeds and being a good person towards others. The world could certainly use a lot more of both. But, the simple fact is Jesus came to earth as a man, lived a perfect life, and went to the cross solely for our benefit as payment for the sins of the entire world. By faith we know all this in our heads and in our hearts. And yet sin for each of us, and me included, is a constant daily struggle. We have to face it and try to overcome it. I am here to tell you that knowing Jesus on a personal level is the only way to overcome sin."

"As precious a thing as it is to know Jesus, I have always found it interesting we don't know what Jesus actually looked like. There are lots of artist renditions in the world. I wonder if having a picture of Jesus implanted in our minds would help us with our struggle to be good Christians, good humans. Please take a look at the screens." David looks back and lifts his arms to both large video screens on both sides of the pulpit to emphasize his point. He continues, "This is my interpretation of what the Son of Man looked like. It's how I see Him, and I hope when you struggle at times with your faith or with troubles at home or work, or when someone cuts you off on the freeway, you can close your eyes and instead of seeing blood and rage will see this image to help you get through tough times, but please don't close your eyes if you're the driver. Wait until it's safe. Or, conjure the image with your eyes open." Laughter spreads across the congregation. David says, "Slow to anger is a biblical concept, but a difficult one to live into in today's world. The image will be available on our church website to download so you have a physical copy whenever you need it at your side. I have a small version I keep in my wallet. I pull it out and stare at it occasionally to help me regain my focus, or calm my mind. I hope it gives each of you a bit of the same peace at the moment in time you need your faith restored or to render more pleasant thoughts on your fellow commuters." David bows his head and waits in silence for the image on the screen to soak in with his congregation. He hears a few murmurs of approval and sees a general nodding of heads in affirmation of the picture's impact. From one section of the sanctuary, one man stands and shouts, "Amen!" After a minute, he continues, "Let us pray…"

After David prays he looks up from the pulpit. His sermon has gone well, and he feels the congregation is in tune with his teaching. The picture of Jesus has brought a strong emotional response. His key point in the sermon was the fact that we knew Jesus existed, we knew His works, but we didn't really know exactly what He looked like. David offers a benediction to close out the service for the evening, "May each of you feel the blessings of the Lord throughout your week. May you come to understand His grace in your life. May you visualize Him and allow Him to lead you to greener pastures. Please, go in peace living each day of the week in His name. Amen."

The sermon is over. The worship leader takes over and starts up a final song of the service as he dismisses the people. David walks off the pulpit down the side aisle of the sanctuary where he is stopped by Bill Martin his executive pastor. Bill is attempting to get David's attention to introduce him to a prominent couple. Bill says, "David Campbell, I would like you to meet Bob and Donna McIntyre. Bob is the vice president of development at a local software firm. They are checking out our church and wanted to meet you personally."

David shakes their hands and smiles warmly, "Welcome to church. I hope you enjoyed the sermon."

Donna complements David, "Pastor, that was a wonderful sermon. I understand the picture of Jesus you showed us was drawn by you! It was a beautiful work of art. It really inspired me and helped me to visualize. Thank you so much. I'm always amazed at how a sermon can touch my heart and seem like it was written just for me in my current situation."

"Thank you, and please call me David."

Bob joined in, "It inspired me as well. And I could tell you were talking directly to me about controlling my road rage!" Bob laughs, "Hopefully now I can have Jesus' image to temper my rage. But seriously, knowing what Jesus looked like would have meant a lot to the world. Why do you suppose He never allowed himself to be drawn?"

David replied, "Only He knows the answer to that question. But I believe a lot of emphasis is placed on faith. After Jesus had risen from the dead, Thomas said he would not believe Jesus had risen until he saw the holes in Jesus' hands and side, and put his finger into the hole. After Jesus appeared to Thomas and allowed him to do these things, Jesus said, 'Thomas, because you have seen Me, you have believed. But, blessed are those who do not see Me, and yet still believe!' So, you raise a good point about..."

As David is talking to the couple, he looks up and sees the woman from his dreams! She is standing at the entrance to the church sanctuary, but has a strange haze surrounding her. She is beckoning him just like his dream, but beginning to fade. Rudely, he interrupts the conversation, and begins to run where the woman was, "Hey you! Wait a minute!" Other people step in front of David and try to compliment him as he moves passed, but his mind is totally occupied, and he doesn't hear them and continues to push through the aisles. When he reaches the foyer, the woman is gone. He looks all around and has a doubting look as if he dreamt the whole thing. Suddenly, as David regains his composure, he realizes people are staring at him and wondering what in the world is going on with their senior pastor. A woman asks him, "Is there something wrong Pastor Campbell? You act like you've seen a ghost or something."

David is consumed with the vision, but he finally comes around. He sees and hears the people around him. They continue to stare. "No. Nothing... I'm sorry." Embarrassed, David turns and hurriedly goes to his office while Bill tries to settle down the people in the lobby.

David sits down at his desk and takes a drink from a bottle of water. He picks up his family picture and stares at it. David looks out the window of his office and sees a hummingbird flitting around the bushes and flowers. His wings are beating at 60 miles per hour and are a blur to David's eyes. The hummingbird floats close to the window and hovers there, just a few feet from him. David stares and wonders and says to no-one in particular, "Now there is something to marvel. Talk about a simple purpose in life. If only..." There is a knock on David's door. After the scene in the sanctuary, he is expecting Bill Martin, but instead after acknowledging the knock, a tall middle-aged man enters the office.

"Pastor, I am sorry to bother you, but do you have a few minutes to talk?"

David flips through the Rolodex in his brain until he locks on to this man's card. They have a fairly large membership, but David prides himself in knowing every church member. He is certain the one attribute he will always keep in his church, even as it grows, is the fact that it is a relationship-based fellowship.

David replies, "Marcus, please come in and have a seat. How is Carolyn?"

Marcus clears his throat and says, "Oh she's fine! I don't want to take up too much of your time. I just came to let you know I was laid off at the plant yesterday. I guess I was lucky to last as long as I did through four separate downsizing cuts in the past year. Carolyn and I were hoping and praying things would turn around."

"Oh Marcus," David replies compassionately, "I'm so sorry. This economy has a lot of families struggling right now. Are you okay financially?"

"We'll be okay for a couple months, but I don't know where to turn for another job. Nobody seems to be hiring right now. It's getting really scary out there!" says Marcus.

David takes it all in and responds assuringly, "Well we'll certainly pray for you and Carolyn as a staff, and I'll make some discreet inquiries from a few members who might have something in the works, or know someone. A little networking never hurts."

Marcus answers, "We would be most grateful for the prayers and the networking." He rises to leave and shakes David's hand. Just as he is about to leave, Bill Martin knocks and opens the door. Marcus steps past Bill to leave and bill says, "Oh, excuse me Marcus, I didn't realize anyone was inside with David. I hope I didn't interrupt."

"Not at all Bill," Marcus replies, "I had just finished my conversation and was about to head home. You have a good evening." Marcus leaves and closes the door behind him. There is tension in the air between David and Bill. Bill breaks the ice, "is everything alright with Marcus and Carolyn?"

David, somewhat icily says, "No! Marcus was laid off from work, and right now he has no prospects. He's a bit scared. We'll want to add his prayer request to our staff prayers."

Bill says, "I'm really sorry to hear that."

"But that's not why you are here, is it?" David replies.

"No it's not. I'm sorry about Marcus, but honestly David, that had to be the rudest thing I've ever seen you do earlier! What was with the exit act? The McIntyre's are important people in the community. They donate a lot of money to charity, and would really like them to become members here! You can't just behave like..."

David interrupts him and speaks as if he didn't hear any of Bill's comments, "Bill, did you see a strange woman in the back of the sanctuary? She was wearing a white flowing robe, and she was beckoning me to come to her?"

Bill, a bit put off by the interruption, responds, "No, I didn't. I looked up when you ran away, and I didn't see anything out of the ordinary except my lead pastor running down the aisle pushing people aside. What in the world came over you?"

David continues almost trancelike, "I can't really explain it fully, but that woman keeps reappearing at odd times. I just need to find her and make contact."

"Odd? That's a strange way of putting it. I thought the way you bolted from the sanctuary was extremely odd, and it really upset a lot of people, me included." Bill continues, but as if not even hearing him, David stands up and starts to gather his stuff and starts to leave by walking past Bill. David continues without responding. Bill stands up and grabs David by the arm before he can leave his office. David turns to him angrily. Bill says, "Wait a minute! Aren't you even going to answer me? You haven't even responded to one of my questions! Is something troubling you? And why are you asking about a woman from the congregation? That has all the signs of **Trouble** spelled with a CAPITAL T!"

David finally comes out of his trance, and stares back at Bill, "No it's not like that at all. She wasn't a normal congregation member. I'd tell you where I have seen her before, but then you would know I was crazy, and probably have me committed to an asylum. Please don't worry, it's nothing to be concerned about. I'll be okay in the morning."

Bill isn't convinced and says, "David, we've been friends for a long time now. I can still remember the first time I met you in seminary. You carried yourself with such flair and poise. I knew someday you'd be doing amazing things in a great church. Well, here we are twenty years later, doing those amazing things in this great church that you and I built together." Bill raises his voice a bit, "Now, don't tell me you've got something happening in your life that doesn't concern me. Everything about you concerns me, and this church! After everything we've been through together, I have a right to know!"

Now, angry himself, David pulls himself away from Bill and states, "Don't pursue this Bill! This is my personal business. It doesn't concern you or the church! So, excuse me while I exercise my right for a little privacy!"

David pulls himself away from Bill and leaves the office. Bill, stands there a bit stunned and in disbelief. Outside David gets into his car. He has successfully avoided any further encounters with people from the evening service. As David drives away, he hesitates at an intersection. To the left lies home, Kathleen and Patty. To the right, the city's downtown district. He remembers Kathleen's request to be home right after church to have dinner with a neighborhood couple. His satchel holding his drawing materials and sketchbook is in the passenger seat. David has pulled the picture of his night time dream and laid it on top of the stack. He picks up the picture, studies it and sets it back down on the passenger seat. He starts to head left towards home, stops, backs up and goes right towards the city.

Back at David's house, the doorbell rings. Kathleen looks at her watch, and is slightly annoyed that David is not home yet. She opens the door, acknowledges the couple standing in the doorway and says, "Hi, thanks for accepting our invitation! Please come in!"

Dan and Brittany Landing walk through the threshold and take off their coats. Dan smiles, "Hello, Thank you so much for inviting us over. We love the neighborhood so far, and really appreciate the opportunity to get together to know you and David better."

Kathleen adds, "David's not home from the church yet, but I expect him any moment. Let me take your coats and get you something to drink. Can I start you off with a glass of wine?"

"I would love a glass of chardonnay if you have it," Brittany says as the three of them head into the living room. Kathleen pauses to look down the street in hopes of seeing David's car approaching, but can only see darkness.

CHAPTER 3

A FACE ON THE CITY

"If anyone acknowledges that Jesus is the son of God, God lives in them and they in God." 1 John 4:15 NIV

David's journey takes him downtown. It is a rundown part of the city. There are a lot of closed down shops and empty warehouses mixed in with some retail spaces. David finds a spot to park the car. He grabs his sketchpad and leaves his car. He is walking down the street when he looks up. Standing in a doorway, he sees the same woman from his dreams. She is staring at him and holding out her arms. A wave of emotions flood his consciousness. David, totally fixated on the woman starts to cross the street toward her, and shouts, "Hey you!"

David is so focussed on the woman he is nearly run over by a bus, and David falls backward in shock. He picks up his drawing materials, looks up only to see the woman has vanished again. David shakes himself off and continues down the street. He rounds a corner. There are homeless people all around. He is approached by one man who grabs David by the arm. In a desperate voice he asks him, "Can you spare some change, man? I need to get something to eat."

David has some small bills in his wallet, but instead says, "I don't have any change on me. I wish I could help." David breaks free from the man's grip and starts to walk away hoping his answer will suffice. As he turns another corner, he stops to see a homeless woman with her daughter staring straight up at him. Their clothes are dirty and ragged. They are clearly malnourished, and it tugs at his heart. He pulls a sheet of paper out of his sketchpad and asks, "Hello, would you allow me to sketch you and your daughter? I would be glad to give you some money to help you in exchange."

The woman replies, "Thank you, that would be very kind of you, and unexpected especially at this hour."

David pulls out his wallet and hands the woman all of his cash, a ten-dollar bill and two ones. He begins to draw. A close up of David's drawing hand shows veins rising and falling and his fingers moving with dexterity as the drawing takes shape. He looks at the girl, then back down at his sketch. As he finishes the drawing, he pushes the heel of his hand in several places to add shadowing and effects that bring the drawing to life. His concentration is so acute that he loses track of time. After a while, he looks up and realizes it has been several minutes. He says to the woman, "Thank you for allowing me to draw you."

The woman replies, "Thank you for your kindness. May I see the picture before you go?"

"Of course," David hands her the drawing.

"This is quite remarkable in such a short amount of time."

David takes the picture back and turns to leave. "I wish there was more I could do for you and your daughter, but I have to go now."

The woman smiles, "You have been much kinder than most. May God bless you!"

David stops for a moment, considers a response, then leaves abruptly. The woman never sees the tears that have welled up in David's eyes.

Back at David and Kathleen's home, Patty and Kathleen are at the front door saying goodnight to their dinner guests. Kathleen says, "Thank you for coming. I'm so sorry David couldn't make it. I'm sure he got tied up with business at the church. There are always so many things that demand his time."

Brittany shakes her head in a manner saying to not worry about it, and responds, "It's okay Kathleen, really! The dinner was delicious and you made us feel really connected. That's a nice feeling when you are new to a neighborhood. Your daughter, Patty, is precious. We'll have you and David over another time. Please don't give it a second thought. We had a wonderful time."

"That's very gracious of you. Good night," Kathleen says.

Patty adds, "Good night." After the door closes Patty continues, "Mom, what happened to dad tonight? I remember you telling him this morning to be home right after church."

Kathleen trying to sooth her daughter, "I don't know sweetheart. Don't worry, he'll be home soon. He probably got distracted with someone from church and let the time get away from him. Saturdays are hard because people demand so much of your dad's time. I probably should have just re-scheduled. It's late. Just head upstairs and get ready for bed."

As Patty heads to bed, Kathleen mutters under her breath, "I need a drink. David, where in God's name are you?"

An hour later David walks into the house. Kathleen is having her second drink. She looks up as he walks past her down the hallway. It's obvious that she has been crying. She gets up and follows David into the bedroom.

In an angry voice Kathleen begins, "WHERE HAVE YOU BEEN? I have been worried sick about you. I called your cell phone multiple times, but it went straight to voicemail."

"I guess my phone died and I didn't realize it. I went for a walk downtown," David replied.

Still with an edge to her voice, "Downtown? For three hours? What's going on with you? I had... we had dinner plans! I was so embarrassed. I had to make up excuses to our new neighbors to cover for your unexplained absence. You promised me you would come home straight after the evening service. Why the mysterious disappearance?"

"Something happened and I needed to be alone... to draw..."

"To draw? I texted you and called your cell phone multiple times. I called the office and spoke to Bill. You weren't there, and nobody knew where you were! I have been sitting here going half crazy, not knowing where you are! I almost called the police! It's hard enough being a pastor's wife under normal conditions because of the tremendous demands put on you. It leaves precious little personal time for the two of us, but this is way beyond even my limits!"

David realizes the seriousness of his breach, "Kathleen, I'm so sorry. I really am. I know I put you in a tough spot. I had to have some time on my own to figure some things out."

Kathleen still has some points to make, "What is going on with you? You've been acting strange for weeks! Your drawing has become an obsession with you, and I know you've been keeping something from me. We've been married for seventeen years and I think I know when something is bothering you." Kathleen pauses and takes a deep breath. A bit calmer now, "David, please tell me what's happening with you. What's happened? You're keeping something from me and it's a scary feeling! Bill said you asked about a woman... Is there something, or someone you are not telling me about?"

David, answers strongly and defensively, "NO! It's nothing like that!" He lowers his head and begins to sob. Kathleen comes closer and hugs him. They embrace for a minute with David's body shuddering and finally relaxing. David continues, "There's something inside me that's... hurting. It's a dull ache in my soul and it's been building for a long time now. I see sick people every day of my life. I see homeless and hungry children who are tormented by life's daily struggle just to survive one more day. You want to know where I was tonight, and who I was with? Here." He pulls out the drawing of the homeless family and hands it to Kathleen. In silence she looks at the drawing. "Every week, I stand in the pulpit and preach the gospel to affluent people who can't, no won't let themselves grasp what the real ills of this world are. We sit in our comfortable homes, send our kids to comfortable schools, go to our comfortable church, and donate a comfortable portion of our wealth to our church. To what end? I'll tell you to what end... To deceive ourselves into believing we've done all we can, but the homeless still have no place to sleep at night, children are still starving and have no peace, gangs roam neighborhoods to prey on helpless people, and even though I'm the senior pastor of a large affluent church with the power to act, I am left powerless to help these people who live only a few miles away in an area most will not venture into because they are afraid. Either afraid they will be hurt or worse afraid they will be uncomfortable." David points to the woman and daughter in the picture and pauses. He takes a deep breath, lowers his head... "I have reached my breaking point, and I feel like a failure! NO! Worse... A fraud because I can't even help the people in this picture in a meaningful way. My faith is shaken at the core of my being."

Kathleen very low and calm now, "David, I'm so sorry. I had no idea you felt this way. Why didn't you come to me and talk about this?"

David, "I'm so sorry I didn't talk to you about this sooner. I've been carrying this burden inside of me for a few months. I try to shield you and Patty from as much as possible. But you're right. We've been married seventeen years, and if there's one person I should have confided in, it's you. I'm very sorry."

Kathleen reassuringly says, "Honey, you can't carry all of the problems of the world on your two shoulders. That's not fair to you or us. Besides, your church supports missionaries all over the world. You do a lot of wonderful things for our community. You do all of these things because you are the senior pastor of an affluent church!"

David, "It's not enough! It can never be enough! It doesn't even put a dent in the world's problems, let alone the problems here in our own back yard."

Kathleen adds, "I spoke to Bill tonight. I think you need to sit down with him and discuss…"

David cuts her off, "Ha! He's the last person I can talk to about this! He has blinders on to anything other than what will grow the church membership by putting more butts in the seats, or what do we have to do for some member who can donate a large sum of money so they will feel special."

Kathleen, "David, that's not fair! Bill carries a tremendous burden in the operation of the church. It takes a lot of money to run all the ministries you support, and it falls on Bill's shoulders to steer the ship through its difficult course. You've told me a hundred times, you don't know how he manages, but he does. It's never about the money. It's about the church reaching and helping as many people find the gospel as it can. Bill is a compassionate man. He's your best friend and he loves you, and would do anything in the world for you!"

A bit embarrassed by his outburst, David says, "You're right. Thanks, that was unfair, but…" David hesitates, but he knows in his heart he has to tell Kathleen about the dreams, "there's more I need to tell you. It's about the woman Bill mentioned. This is going to sound crazy… it even sounds crazy to me and I'm the one who has been experiencing it for a couple months now. Here it is… I have been having a strange recurring dream just like the one you woke me from this morning. I'm in a desert far away. The dust is blowing all around, and I can just make out a large domed building in the distance, and a wall… Off to my right I see buildings more clearly, and a woman in long flowing white robes is standing there beckoning me to come to her. It is so surreal and at times is happening in slow motion."

33

Kathleen shakes if off and says, "Okay, it's just a dream and it doesn't sound so crazy."

David waves his hands and continues, "NO wait! That was exactly what I thought until tonight. The woman from my dreams, I saw her tonight, standing at the back of the church after my sermon. I know it was her. When I looked up and saw her, I raced up the aisles. But, when I got there, she was gone. It really freaked me out, and unfortunately a few of our members. When I asked about her, nobody else saw her. Then, later this evening when I was out walking, miles away from church, I looked across the street, and there she was standing in a doorway, just staring at me. I started to cross the street, but a bus passed by and cut me off. When it passed, she was gone, almost magically. I don't know if I'm dreaming the whole thing, or if I need to check into a padded room where they make you wear funny white jackets with sleeves that wrap around your body."

Kathleen nods her head trying to understand and grasp what David is telling her. Reassuringly she says, "Wow, that is an intense experience, but I know one thing for certain. You are not crazy. You've been working long hours and haven't been sleeping well. It's very late. Let's see if we can't get some sleep, and we'll talk about it some more in the morning. I know we'll find a way to work through this, together." They reach for each other and embrace. David holds onto her and is comforted by how open and understanding his wife is with him. They head upstairs arm in arm.

Later that evening, David and Kathleen have been asleep for a while. David is caught up in the fullness of his dream again. He's sweaty and tossing in bed. Outside through the bedroom window, the mysterious lady is standing there alone in the night staring into David's window. A breeze is blowing passed her, billowing her robes yet the leaves on the nearby trees stand still. She is staring directly at David's window and appears to the be the one making David have his dream.

The next morning is Sunday morning, and it's a very busy day for David. He heads into church with a lot on his mind. It's still very early and only the worship team and some of the staff have arrived to prepare for the Lord's day. David passes his office and goes to Bill's office. He knocks lightly, steps in and finds a chair in front of Bill.

David starts, "Bill, I'm so sorry about last night. I was way out of line, and I apologize for the way I acted and the things I said to you. You didn't deserve it, again, I apologize."

Bill nods his head in a friendly gesture and says, "Apology accepted." He hesitates a moment pondering how to approach his next few words, "David, we've been friends for a long time and I've never seen you act the way you've been acting the past couple of weeks. Please tell me what is going on with you, so we can fix it, and get things back to normal around here."

David sits and wonders at the word 'normal' and knows nothing about what he has been experiencing would be considered normal or anything close to normal. He wants to just leave and head back to his office to prepare for the day, but replies, "That's just it. I'm not sure I can get back to normal... I haven't felt normal for some time. In fact, I'm thinking about giving it all up. Maybe it's time I just move on to something else. I think I've lost my passion, if not for preaching then for shepherding, or at the very least the heavy responsibility for guiding our flock. I have even been questioning my faith because of this change of heart."

Bill is shocked and cannot contain himself, "What? You can't quit now. We've come so far, and we've done so much. If you quit now, this church will never survive. You are the face of this church, and our congregation relies on you, and your faith to get us through. Not to mention our debt to the bank will be in jeopardy because you're the reason people trust our ministry to manage their tithes to this church!"

David replies, "That's ridiculous! No one person is that crucial to the long-term success of this church."

"Now who's kidding who? You know the financial situation here. The debt to the bank won't pay itself off. Our step out in faith incurred a large financial obligation that will take years to pay off." Bill opens his desk drawer and pulls out a sheet of paper that is obviously crinkled and worn. He holds up the paper to show to David. "Remember our 'deal' from Seminary school? And I quote: 'I build a church to give them a place to come, God will bring them in, and you deliver the sermons to give them a reason to come back.' Signed by, and I quote, David Campbell. Your work here isn't finished yet, my friend. I believe that with all my heart."

"I don't know Bill, and I'm not sure how binding that 'contract' is between us. Lately, I write the sermons, and I say the words, but anymore they leave me feeling hollow inside. It feels like I'm playing a charade with myself, and our congregation. I don't think I can keep doing it."

Bill sits there a second before replying. Inside he is incredulous with David's revelation, but he doesn't want to overreact and say something out of hand that he will regret later. Then he gets an idea, "Let's think this through and not do anything rash. Maybe what you need is to take a break from it all. It sounds like a severe case of 'pastor burn out' to me. You need to get away from it all, and get a fresh perspective on life. I believe a sabbatical is just what the doctor orders to snap you back in shape."

David shakes his head and says, "I don't know Bill, it feels a bit more than that..."

"Hey! Wait a minute," Bill interrupts, "I've got just the thing! Tim Sinclair is leading a three-week archaeological tour of the Holyland? A trip to Jerusalem would do you, Kathleen and Patty a world of good and help to recharge your batteries." David initially has a negative take on the idea, but his mind is switching gears. This might be a very good thing, and the timing couldn't be better! Bill continues, "Take some time off, pray about your situation, re-energize and come home ready to take the reins. I will get some guest speakers to come in and cover for you. We will tell the congregation you are on a sabbatical to refresh yourself and your family. When you get back, we'll have a serious talk about your concerns. If you still feel the same way, then we'll make it work for you, and the church, somehow."

David is thinking about Bill's offer and it does make sense for the reasons he stated, and a couple extra reasons that he won't share with Bill right now. Out of fear? No, not really fear. He just doesn't want to explain all the details of his life right now with his mystery lady. David answers, "Every time we disagree about something, and you want to get your way with me, you pull that old piece of paper out of your drawer. I am pretty sure the statute of limitations has run out. Regardless, one of these days that isn't going to work, my friend." Bill chuckles at his friend. David continues, "Okay, maybe a short time away will clear my head. I'll do it. Thanks Bill. You know... Whenever I think of the tough times we've shared over the past twenty years, you've always been that strong constant support structure for me. We have always been a great partnership, and I have really enjoyed the journey with you. I don't know if this trip holds any answers for me, but somehow God will see us and our church through. Thanks."

CHAPTER 4

A FACE IN THE SKY

"Give thanks to the Lord, for he is good, his love endures forever.." 1 Chronicles 16:34 NIV

David, Kathleen, and Patty are on the airplane headed for Jerusalem. The intercom announces that they will be arriving into the Tel Aviv, Ben Gurion International Airport in less than an hour. Patty is at the window and has a guide and history book. David is finishing drawing a picture of a mother and a baby in the seat in front of him. He hands the picture to the mother.

She replies, "Thank you! It's beautiful, but you didn't sign it!"

David looks over at Patty who smiles back at him. He answers with a smile, "Thank you, but I never sign any of the pictures I create. I consider my art a gift from the Lord and my signature would be an act of self-pride."

"Well thank you just the same," The mother turns and busies herself with her baby as they get closer to their destination.

Kathleen chimes in, "At least you figured out how to spend quality time on a 14-hour flight! I cannot wait to be safely on the ground. The turbulence from a few hours ago left me queasy, and I couldn't sleep a wink while we were flying through it."

David replies, "I have to admit it… my drawing is an all-consuming habit. I hardly noticed the turbulence. I hope you are you excited for our adventure in the Holyland."

"Oh, you have no idea! I have always dreamed about doing this, and honestly, I cannot believe it is actually happening! This trip is exactly what the doctor ordered," Kathleen answered.

David turns to Patty and asks, "How about you? Are you looking forward to the next 4 weeks?"

Patty blushes with excitement, "Oh yes daddy. I have been reading up on some of the locations we will be visiting. It's so exciting. There's so much biblical history everywhere in the country. I can't wait to get started."

A loud beep in the cabin gets everyone's attention. The flight attendant comes on the intercom, "Ladies and gentlemen, we will be landing shortly. Please bring your seat backs to their forward and locked position and close your tray tops. Welcome to Tel Aviv, Israel. We hope you have a wonderful time whether you are on business or traveling for pleasure."

After arriving at the terminal and gathering their luggage, a bus picks them up and drops their tour group off at the King David Hotel in downtown Jerusalem. The hotel was built in 1929 and has been a part of Israel's rich history for a long time including welcoming it to statehood in 1947. It's a magnificent hotel and is just a fifteen minute walk from the

Old City. The Old City is divided into Armenian, Christian, Jewish and Muslim Quarters; the Western Wall; the Dome of the Rock; the Via Dolorosa and the Church of the Holy Sepulcher.

Up in their room, David gathers his sketchpad and drawing materials, puts them in his satchel and exclaims, "Kathleen, I'm going out for a walk. I want to get a little exercise in after sitting on that airplane for so long! Anybody want to tag along?"

Kathleen comes in from the bathroom and in a good natured way replies, "Patty and I are both tired from the trip. We're going to take a nap to get in synch with our jet lag. Is this going to be a quick walk, or one of your special all evening outings?"

David smirks, "Ha, very funny! I'll try to be back before the full moon changes me completely!" David's dreams had continued to occur, but he had not had another sighting of the mystery woman since church and downtown. The dreams had continued to reveal new features each time, and David would make small adjustments to his drawing after awaking from the dream.

Kathleen, a bit more seriously, "Just remember, Tim has scheduled the tour to start very early tomorrow morning, and you'll need to get some rest."

David leaves the hotel room. Next he is leaving the hotel. He turns a couple of corners. He hasn't traveled far when he comes across a homeless man and woman begging for money. In Hebrew they ask for help.

The man speaks, "האם אתה יכול לעזור לנו בבקשה?"

David doesn't understand, but knows they are in need. He reaches into his pocket and pulls out a twenty Shekel note. He hands the money to the man and says, "Shalom."

The man replies, "Toda Raba."

David asks, "Do you speak any english?"

"A little bit," the man answers.

David continues, "Do you mind if I draw a picture of you and your spouse?"

The man considers the question trying to understand the request. David holds up his sketchpad and materials. The man shakes his head approvingly as it dawns on him what David is asking. "It will be okay," he manages. David sets up to start drawing. After a moment the man brokenly asks, "'why would you want draw pictures of us poorly persons?

David continues to sketch and thinks about the man's question. He finally replies, "I'm not sure really. I like to draw pictures of people with emotion, and I find the people in the street have their emotions out on display much more than other people. There's a simple truth in drawing pictures of poor people that says, 'here I am, all of me' and I find that refreshing. There is a raw truth for me to draw in this setting. Do you understand?"

The man answers in broken English, "No, but it first time anyone ever draw my wife and I."

After David finishes the drawing, he packs up his materials. He hands the man a second twenty shekel note and continues down the street. He moves around a corner when David looks up and sees the mystery woman in the distance beckoning him. He shouts to her, "Are you serious? Here? What do you want from me? Why won't you leave me alone?"

David is near several people when he shouts his questions. One man stops and speaks to David in heavily accented English, "I beg your pardon. Who are you talking to?"

David is distracted by the man. He looks at him and points in the direction of his ghostly encounter, "What? I'm trying to figure out why that woman over there has followed me half way around the world!"

The man looks in the general direction where David is pointing, but sees no one in particular. "I'm sorry sir, but to what woman are you referring?"

David has looked away from his woman stalker to answer the man and looks back to see the mystery woman has disappeared again. He shakes his head in frustration, and bewilderment, "Um… Nobody. I'm very sorry to have bothered you."

The man watches David with a strange look as David starts to leave. He shakes his head and walks off in the opposite direction.

The close encounter has shaken David so he decides to return to the hotel and re-group. When he arrives at the room, Kathleen is coming out of the bathroom. She is immediately happy to see David has returned, "That was pretty quick! How was your walk? Meet and draw any interesting people?"

David still shaken by the experience says, "In a manner of speaking I have! I've just seen my mystery lady again, and for the life of me I can't figure out what is going on! The moment I looked away, she disappeared again. I had to pinch myself to make sure I wasn't dreaming, and to make sure I was real. This woman or apparition follows me half way around the world. You'd think she would have the decency to speak a word or two to me, and not just disappear again in the blink of an eye!"

Kathleen comes over and hugs David tightly, reassuringly, "Why don't you go in, take a nice hot shower and get some rest? You always tell me that God reveals His purpose for our lives in His own time. Maybe you just need to relax, and let even this mystery unfold in its own time."

"Well," David says, "if I'm as smart as I think I am, maybe my own advice will work... even for me."

The next morning, true to his word, Tim has the group in a tour bus heading out for the day's journey. They have visited the Wailing Wall, and are now driving down a cobbled road a couple miles outside the city center. Tim continues his lecture on the bus, "Jerusalem's unique position among cities of the world derives from its crucial role in religious history as a holy city for three great monotheistic religions: Judaism, Christianity, and Islam. For thousands of years Jerusalem has been the temporal and spiritual center of the Holy Land, for which more tears and blood have been shed and more prayers offered than for any other region of the world. Jerusalem's powerful emotional appeal has inspired a prodigious outpouring of prose and poetry, artistic renderings, and, of course, maps. In about 1004 BC King David conquered the small Jebusite city of Jerusalem, fortified it, renamed it The City of David, and established it as the capital of the first united Jewish kingdom from Samuel 2 chapter 5, verses 4 through 12." Patty raises her hand to gain Tim's attention, "yes Patty, did you have a question?"

Patty asks, "What is the domed building in the background of the Wailing Wall?"

Tim thinks for a second and answers, "The gold dome, or Dome of the Rock, is the first Muslim masterpiece and was built in 687 AD by Caliph Abd al-Malik, half a century after the death of the Prophet Muhammad. Muslims believe that Muhammad was carried to heaven from here by the angel Gabriel. In Jewish tradition Abraham was said to have prepared to sacrifice his son Isaac at the site. That is the heart of why Jerusalem is the center for the three religions, Muslim, Judaism, and Christianity. We'll stop just up ahead where there's a wonderful view of the Dome of the Rock."

After another climb the bus stops, and the tour group exits to take in the latest sites. David, Kathleen and Patty are still on the bus and David looks at Patty. He says, "Patty, you've been pretty quiet all day. What do you think of your tour of the Holyland so far?"

Patty smiles back at her dad, "Israel is such a beautiful country. There's so much history here, it's overwhelming. You always see and hear about problems in the middle east on TV, but it's so peaceful it seems as if they must be talking about another country far away, and not about this land."

David nods his head, "The media tends to explode every issue into a media event. Actually, we have much more crime and violence in America on a daily basis. It just isn't as newsworthy as the events that happen here. A lot of the more recent turmoil has been centered in Iraq and Syria. Hopefully, the peace process will continue, so we will see less and less of the violence. Of course, I'm not sure what the media will have to report on when peace finally does arrive!"

"Oh dad! Sometimes you can be so cynical," Patty replies with a grin, "last one out is a rotten egg!" The three of them scramble to exit the bus, but Patty beats them outside. They walk over to where people are in awe of the sight. Many have taken out their cameras and are snapping away. As David approaches the site, he looks up and he cannot believe what is unfolding before his eyes. He is seeing the view from his dreams come to life! It is the exact view from his dreams except it has the gold domed building in a slightly different angle. It is a startling revelation because David has never been to this place before. He takes a few steps forward, but feels faint and almost stumbles. David stops and closes his eyes. The scene from his dream comes to life. It is virtually the same except now it's real and not a hazy dream. David slowly opens his eyes and shakes his head in disbelief.

Kathleen notices her husband's shakiness and asks, "David are you alright? You look as if you've seen a ghost."

David pulls up his sketchpad and shuffles through his pictures until he stops on the drawing from his dream. He holds the drawing out to Kathleen and says, "I think maybe I have. Take a look at this and tell me I'm not crazy after all. I drew this weeks ago, before I even knew this place existed! It's as if I've drawn it before the Dome of the Rock ever existed and that was thirteen hundred years ago!"

Kathleen just shakes her head in confusion. She's desperate to give David a logical answer to his dilemma, but she is just as dumbfounded. Finally, she offers, "David this is really fantastic. Is this the picture you were hiding from me the other morning in the kitchen? I noticed you swap it out to show me Patty's picture, but I knew you were keeping something from me."

"Yes, I wasn't sure how to tell you about my visions then. At least you know I'm not crazy. Now the only question is why am I constantly being bombarded with this imagery?"

Kathleen looks over at Tim and asks, "Tim, those ruins off to the right, what are they, or should I say, what were they?"

Tim responds to Kathleen, "Thanks Kathleen. That was a perfectly timed question! We believe it was a cultural center and marketplace on the outskirts of Jerusalem over 2000 years ago. We'll be traveling down there and going through the ruins. There are many chambers and caverns. Most of the ruins are still buried under tons of earth. Archaeologists believe there are significant undiscovered artifacts all around the area dating back to the time when Jesus was alive."

David is pondering the meaning of his vision and this site. He mutters mostly to himself and his mystery lady, "So, this is what you wanted me to see. But, why? What does it all mean?"

Kathleen hears him mutter and asks, "I'm sorry David. I couldn't hear what you said..."

The tour group starts to re-board the bus to head to the ruins. David turns and says, "Nothing, let's go!"

The bus pulls up to the ruins and people shuffle out. The ruins extend several hundred yards into the side of a hill. The tour group gathers around Tim. Tim gives them a little speech about what they are going to see. "These ruins were a thriving part of Jerusalem about 2000 years ago. Massive sand storms covered up the majority of the site over a long period of time. They extend into the hillside where several caves have been dug to excavate the remaining ruins. Please stay close together inside the caves because they branch out at different times and we don't want anyone getting lost. Everyone grab a flashlight and a bottle of water."

The tour group heads out with David following in the back of the group. He's looking around nervously as if waiting for the mystery lady to appear! The group heads into the ruins. They travel a small distance and then head into a section of ruins that have been excavated. David is following near the rear of the group, and stops to make a quick sketch of an interesting plant. After he finishes, he hurries to catch the group. As the group rounds a corner, David catches a glimpse of a bright light from the corner of his eye. He sees a flash of his mystery woman disappearing around a corner. David veers off towards the light and rounds the corner. He sees her rounding another corner and David increases his speed to catch up. He comes to a ledge, but he can't quite make out the lighted object, so he jumps down about 4 feet to get a closer look. As he hits, the ground beneath his feet gives way and he crashes through the earth. He is met with a swirling of wind and dust and flashing lights. In a hazy almost incoherent way, David feels like he is caught in the tornado that picks up Dorothy and her house from the *Wizard of Oz*. There is such a sense of speed and the world is spinning out of control. Finally, just like in that magical land of Oz, he lands with a crash. The last thing David remembers is feeling excruciating pain in his head and his shoulder, and just before he passes out, he sees a man's face.

David awakens. He is on a bedroll. He starts to get up, but the pain in his head and shoulder stops him. David reaches for his head and feels a bandage covering a very sore spot where he hit his head during his fall. He also has a bandage covering his shoulder. He notices that he is dressed strangely. His clothes are loose fitting draped garments. A man walks into the small bedroom dressed similarly. He speaks in heavily accented English.

Joshua looks at David and shakes his head. He says, "I see you are finally awake! How are you feeling, my friend? You had a nasty fall!"

David does another self-check and replies, "Fine except for a massive headache and a stiff shoulder. What happened? Where am I? Where are my clothes?"

Joshua answers, "You came crashing through my roof wearing the clothes you are now wearing. How you got up there, and what you were doing, I cannot say. My name is Joshua, and this is my carpentry shop, and my home. My wife, Rebecca, went for a doctor, and should be returning at any moment."

David looks around. It isn't much more than a hovel with sparse furnishings. He is really confused and is trying to focus on Joshua's revelations, "My name is David Campbell. Thank you for you and your wife's kindness. What do you mean, I crashed through your roof? I need to reach my wife." David reaches around his body looking for his cell phone. Pain stops him when he tries to reach with his right arm. He asks, "I seem to have lost my cell phone. Is there a telephone nearby that I can use?"

This question adds to Joshua's confusion, "Te-le-fone? I know of no such thing. I was working at my bench over there when you just dropped through the ceiling. You can still see the hole in my roof, and the mess that remains where you landed. I will lose a whole day's work fixing my roof. What were you doing up there?"

The confusion for both men remains unresolved. David wonders how much time has passed and where Kathleen and the tour group might be. "What time is it? Where is my wristwatch?"

Joshua scratches his head as the strangeness continues, "'Rist-Watch?' These words you use are strange to me. I am sorry, but I cannot answer you. As for the time, it is a couple hours before sunset and the Sabbath. Maybe you should rest some more while we wait for the doctor."

David turns to sit up and stand. He gets up off of the bedroll and looks closer at some of the objects. All the while Joshua is keeping a close eye on him. David picks up what looks like a cane or walking stick. He says, "This is excellent craftsmanship! Your attention to detail is remarkable. Is all of this work crafted by hand?"

"I know of no other way then by my own skilled hands which thank you for your complement," Joshua says. Joshua picks up David's sketchpad. Joshua states, "I found this collection of drawings near where you fell. I am equally impressed at your skills as an artist as well! What is this place? It is quite remarkable. There is no mountain around here of that shape." Joshua has pulled out a picture David drew of the Matterhorn at Disneyland.

David chuckles a bit and answers, "I'm surprised! I thought everyone knew about the Matterhorn. My family spent our last vacation there. You've never seen a picture of the Matterhorn before?"

Joshua shakes his head no, "Again, you speak of strange places and things of which I have no knowledge. It is beautifully drawn with a master's skill."

David wants to leave and go find his family and tour group, but doesn't want to appear selfish or ungrateful. It's funny, they are both artists in their own way, and they connect over their skills, but something is out of place. David tells Joshua, "you may have the drawing if it pleases you as a thanks for patching up my head and shoulder. Now, I have to find my tour group and my family. My wife will be getting worried. Can you please help?"

Joshua says, "Thank you. I can only give you directions once I know where it is you wish to go." At that moment, Joshua's wife Rebecca walks into the room with the doctor.

Rebecca says, "Are you feeling all right? You hit your head pretty hard. I put the dressing on it as best I could, but felt you should be looked at by a doctor. I am Rebecca, Joshua's wife and this is Solomon, our doctor."

Joshua adds, "He keeps speaking of strange places and things. He must have hit his head harder than we thought. Or, maybe what he needs is a Rabbi instead of a doctor. Haha."

David adds, "Hello, my name is David, and it has been a long day. I just want to find my family, and get back to my hotel."

Joshua, "Do you see what I mean? 'Ho-tel?' So many strange things come from his mouth."

Solomon motions David to sit down, and he looks over his head. Next, he looks at his arm and shoulder. Solomon says, "Well, let's have a look and see if there is anything serious." As Dr. Solomon lifts David's arm, he winces in pain. Solomon continues, "You don't appear to have any broken bones. Just the same, I would keep the arm..." Solomon puts his fist under David's armpit and pulls abruptly on David's arm. The shoulder was dislocated and Solomon skillfully resets it as David screams out in absolute pain! Solomon continues his sentence, "... in a sling, and rest it for a day or so. There, the shoulder was dislocated. I have set the bone back in its socket and now it has a chance to heal properly."

It takes a moment for the pain to subside. David stands back up. He grabs his drawing materials, and starts to head to the entrance, "I can't rest now! I have to get out of here and find my family! I will just hail a taxi to take me back to the King David Hotel! Thank you again for your kindness!"

Dr. Solomon, Rebecca and Joshua stand by without stopping David. Joshua speaks up first, "Taxi? See! I told you he needed a rabbi, not a doctor. You don't suppose he truly <u>thinks</u> he is a <u>king</u>? If that is the case, even a rabbi will not be enough. He must have really hit his head harder than we knew!"

CHAPTER 5

A FACE IN DANGER

"Do not overcome evil with evil, but overcome evil with good."
Romans 12:21 NIV

David steps outside the room and is immediately struck with both awe and confusion. The streets are filled with strangely dressed people. It is a marketplace and there are live animals running around. The smells are overwhelming! David starts walking down the dirt street, turning and staring at the strange sites. The buildings are clustered together and made with a combination of wood and clay. The roofs are thatched with straw and mud. David wonders what in the world has happened. The knock on his head has disoriented him somehow, and he feels like he is in some elaborate dream. He mutters, "Where am I? What is going on?" He walks down one street, and is amazed by the sites. David approaches one of the street vendors who is selling baskets. "Can you tell me how I can get to downtown Jerusalem?"

The man replies, "You **are** in the center of town. Do you want to buy one of my fine baskets? Woven from the finest materials..."

David continues his questions, "No, thank you. I need to get to the King David Hotel. Can you help me?"

The man grows more impatient, "I do not understand what it is you want. If you don't want to buy a basket please move along and make room for another."

David is starting to panic and he raises his voice to the man. He grabs the man by his robes. "You don't understand! I have to find my family!" The man pushes David away. As David stumbles backwards, he falls into the back of a soldier. The soldier turns around, punches David in the face and pushes him to the ground. He lands on his bad arm and shoulder and screams out loud in agonizing pain. David looks up and sees a man wearing what appears to be a bronze tarnished helmet. His top is worn leather with rivets in the seams. The breastplate has an eagle emblem. Leather straps hang down from his waist to just below his knees. A sword is strapped to his belt. David slowly rises, "who are you?" The soldier pulls his sword from the scabbard, "I am a centurion guard. What is going on here? Why have you lunged at me, Hebrew?"

The basket weaver answers, "We mean nothing against you. This strange man accosted me. He appears to be irrational and is behaving very strangely. I can only attribute it to the bandage on his head."

David replies, "I told this gentleman, I am lost and trying to find my way back to the Jerusalem archaeological ruins, and find my family and tour group."

"See what I told you?" The man states, "I already told him he is in Jerusalem, and yet he continues to speak strangely."

The centurion grabs David by his sore arm, "I think you should come with me for additional questioning." David screams out in pain and pulls away. He cannot fathom what is happening to him and he feels completely lost. He begins to run and rounds a corner of a small shack. Unfortunately, he runs straight into another centurion guard. When the first centurion catches up to him, he grabs David by the robes and knocks him down again. "What is the matter with you Hebrew scum? You should have picked this day to stay inside because now you can spend your precious Sabbath locked up and in chains!"

The second centurion adds, "After ten lashes from my whip, but I would wager you won't be conscious after five."

The centurion grabs the satchel with the drawing materials and escorts David to an open area within the prison walls. They tie him up to a tall post that has a chain ring near the top. The post has dried blood all around it, and has a smell of carnage that assaults David's nostrils. They pull David's top off exposing his bare back. The centurion stands back about six feet and pulls his whip off of his belt. "I'm feeling gracious today Hebrew, and will only give you eight lashes from my whip."

David pulls on his wrists to no avail, "I don't understand why you are doing this to me. I am an American and have rights even in this country!"

The centurion responds, "I do not know what your issues are Hebrew, but you will learn to respect your Roman hosts. Accosting a centurion is the same as attacking the governor himself." And with that statement he pulls back and cracks the whip down onto David's back and around to his ribcage. A hot searing pain pummels through David and he screams out in anguish. Without hesitation, the second, third and fourth lashes flail at David and tear through the skin on his back. David's head is hanging as he tries to breathe through the pain. His whole body has gone limp. Lashes five, six and seven happen in a blur. There is extreme pain with each stroke. By the eighth lashing David has passed out!

"I must be losing my touch. He didn't pass out until the seventh lash," says the centurion.

The captain of the guard, Aurelius, comes out to see what has brought in two of his guards, and to discover the reason for whipping and imprisoning a local citizen. Aurelius asks, "What is the charge for this one?"

The first centurion is winding up his whip while the second one is pulling David's robe back over his back. He answers, "general unrest in the marketplace. He assaulted one of his own people and lunged at us. He doesn't appear to be right in the head. When he resisted, we arrested him and brought him in for his punishment."

Aurelius, "Did anyone claim him, or try to come to his aid?"

"No, there was no-one around him," replied the first centurion.

They hand Aurelius the satchel containing the drawing sketchpad, "he had only this on him. He appears to be an artist." Aurelius flips through the pages of the sketchpad. He admires the work and wonders at some of the strangeness of the drawings with large structures that are very foreign looking. Even his knowledge of buildings back in Rome do not look like these structures.

Aurelius nods, "Try to get the details of who he is and where he resides once he wakes up. For now, toss him in a cell with his fellow criminal tribesmen." He hands the sketchpad back to his guards.

The centurions grab David roughly, and half carry, half drag him inside the prison cell blocks. They dump him in a cell with six other men. They take his satchel with the sketchpad back to the main office and put it on a table. After the guards leave, two men come over to David and try to wake him. They revive him to a semi-conscious state. One of the men asks his name and what he did to be whipped and imprisoned. David in a low and pained tone replies, "I have no idea what I did to deserve this. I am lost and do not know how I got to this strange place. I keep hoping this is some dream or nightmare and hope to awaken back in my comfortable bed, but every sense within my broken body tells me this is real, and I am trapped within. My name is David. What did you do to earn your place in this purgatory?"

"Each of us has fought our Roman occupiers in various small ways. Many more have been put to death for stronger acts of resistance. They are a mighty occupational force, and I fear our nation will be enslaved for a long time to come. We have prayed to God for a long time to save us, but so far his response has been only silence."

A realization starts to come into David's mind, but the thought is too incredulous. Even thinking about it makes his sore head ache even more. David decides to try and get some rest. All he can do is lay on his stomach because it feels as if his back has been turned into hamburger. The thought of trying to roll over makes him sick to his stomach. The pain is unrelenting and pulsates throughout his whole body. David finally nods off for a couple of hours of pain interrupted sleep.

A slight clinking sound wakes David. For the briefest of moments he hopes and prays he will awaken from his personal nightmare, but the pain on his back tells him that his state of affairs has not improved. He turns to the cell door as it creaks open and a woman's head peers through with a candle. David wearily looks up to see, of all people, the woman from his dreams! She is dressed similarly to his dreams. Normally this would have appeared out of place, but that is how everyone is now dressed. David looks at her in awe and says in a low voice, "This day just keeps getting better and better!"

The woman walks into the cell and shushes David. She whispers, "You must be very quiet, and do exactly as I say, or we will never escape from here with our lives."

The woman has David's satchel and sketchpad slung over her shoulder. She sets them down momentarily and helps David to his feet. He moans as he stands. David whispers, "How did you find my drawings? Who are you? How did you open the cell door?"

The woman shushes him again and harshly answers, "Please! Not now! My name is Mary. I will explain once we are free of this prison. If we are caught, it will mean death for both of us!" This last statement quiets David. Mary leads David past the six sleeping prisoners and then four guards in the outer area. They walk through several doors that should be locked, but the woman opens them with ease. As they exit the prison building, she extinguishes her candle. Moonlight is the only source of light outside. A few candles can be seen in windows, but other than these scarce sources of light, the town is completely dark. The only sounds are crickets and the occasional dog barking in the distance.

David asks, "Where are you taking us?"

The woman hisses back, "Not NOW! Just follow me."

"If it wasn't for the fact that I have seen you so many times in the past few weeks," David adds, "and I have a strong aversion to prison cells and guards with whips, I wouldn't be following you at all."

She gives David an angry glance, "Please stop talking. We must hurry now! Can you go any faster?"

David nods and says, "I can try... and thank you!"

They continue to walk and the woman gives David as much support as she can. She knows his back is in bad shape because the blood has soaked through his garment. She lets him support himself on her shoulder. As they round the corner of a building, they almost run straight into a centurion guard. She ducks them into a dark corner. The wall is rough and David suppresses a moan as his back rubs against the wall. The centurion turns in their direction hearing something but quite knowing where the sound came from or from how far off. He walks toward them and passes by. He pauses just past where they are ensconced in the shadows. He hears some more noises in the distance, but guesses it was a rat or a dog scrounging for food. David and the strange woman move on. They continue for another few minutes, and manage to avoid any further close encounters with more centurions. Finally, they reach their destination, and the woman opens a door and they go inside. She helps David over to a bed and sets him down to sit. Then, she goes over and puts her ear on the door and listens for any outside activity. She doesn't hear anything alarming and for the first time in over three hours, she lets out a sigh of relief.

David in a low voice asks, "What are you doing?"

She replies, "I'm listening for anyone who might have followed us!" She walks away from the door and goes to sit down. There is a pitcher of water on the table. She pours two glasses of water and hands one to David. "It looks like we made it. I was as scared as I have been for a long time. I thought for sure that one centurion would discover us hiding in the shadows. Another miracle for sure!"

David starts to ramble, "This has been the worst day of my life. Let me recap. I've crashed through a roof I was never on to get a dislocated shoulder and a concussion. I ran into a soldier with an attitude, who decides to use my face as a punching bag, and my back as a rug for 10 lashes from his whip. Next, I'm left for dead in a prison cell. A woman who I have dreamt about for over a month who, until now, was just a figment of my imagination, comes and miraculously performs a prison break that would make Harry Houdini jealous. Everyone is dressed strangely... including myself. There are animals everywhere, no paved roads, no telephones, and no electric lights. I would ask you to pinch me to see if I am dreaming, but I'm in too much pain.

Mary is a bit confused by everything David is saying, "I'm not sure what all of that means. You speak about so many strange things. But, my master sent me to you. He gave me explicit instructions to enter the prison. He said all of the guards and prisoners would be asleep, and all the cell doors would open freely. He told me to follow the light to your cell, get your drawings, and to help you escape. He also told me to wait here for his disciples before bringing you to him. It happened exactly as he said it would. So, even though I was scared for my life and yours too, for me, it is another miracle among many that continues to solidify my faith in him."

David is listening to her story completely spellbound, "who is your master, and how would he know all of that?"

Mary continues, "Jesus of Nazareth is my Lord. He saved me from being stoned to death, and I have followed him ever since. My faith in him grows daily, and I have given my life in his service. I do not understand how he knows what he knows. I am bound to follow him, and do as he instructs in all matters. I would give my life for him, and know in my heart he would do the same for me."

David has a strange look on his face. The reality of what is happening and where he is, is now more than just conjecture. The incredulous becomes a reality. It doesn't come close to answering the millions of other questions formed in David's mind. Almost as a knee-jerk response he asks, "Is this some sort of joke?"

Mary angrily responds, "I assure you, it is no joke. I take everything my master tells me very seriously. How else could you explain the miracle of your escape at the hands of those Romans? I found you exactly as my master predicted. This is not a joking matter and I would certainly never risk my life for a joke!"

As David contemplates everything that has transpired over the past twenty-four hours, he begins to accept the fact that he has miraculously traveled back in time to first century Jerusalem, "As crazy as all of this is, I'm beginning to understand my situation. I'm not sure if I believe all of it because it is simply too fantastic to consider. There are no electric lights, no paved streets, no cars, no telephones, and everyone is dressed strangely! But, how is this possible?"

Mary replies, "To my eyes, everything is normal. I do not understand why it is not to you. But, all things are possible through my master. I've witnessed many miracles at his hands. To me, you are simply his latest. If all of this is strange to you, then some part of his plan has yet to be revealed to you. I assure you, it will unfold at the appropriate time and place of his choosing."

David is settling down from the shock of the prison, but now his excitement rises at this latest revelation, "I'm beginning to believe you, but this really is a miracle in more ways than even you can realize! When can we go to Jesus? I must see him."

"As I said earlier, we are to wait for more of his disciples to arrive. They will have further instructions and will take us to Jesus when the time is right. For now, let me look at your wounds, dress them, and then we'll get some rest." Mary approaches David and removes his tattered and blood-soaked robe. She studies his back trying to determine how deep some of the lacerations go. "I need to attend to these wounds. Some of them are quite deep. I don't want them to get infected." She gets a bowl of water and begins to dress David's wounds. David winces at the treatment. Mary continues, "I am sorry, but they have given you just enough of their so-called justice that I need to wash and dress your wounds. We would not want them to fester and cause you further problems. You will definitely have scars after these wounds heal. Their savagery is boundless. You are lucky to be alive. Many of my fellow Hebrews have died from the Roman whip. Hold tight as this will sting a bit."

David thinks back through the day again and remembers his meeting with the doctor, "my wincing is merely my way of saying thank you! At least this doesn't hurt as bad as Solomon fixing my dislocated shoulder! What a day!"

"Solomon, our local doctor? You have already met him?" Mary asks.

"Yes. He attended to my dislocated shoulder and my head. The lashing from the centurion takes the prize for most painful, but resetting a dislocated shoulder comes in a close second! I am afraid I left Joshua's home in rather a hurry and in quite a confused state. They are probably wondering where such a strange man could come from especially since I came crashing through his roof!"

Mary finishes cleaning and dressing the lash marks left by the centurion's whip. A couple of the lashes tore at the flesh pretty deeply. She applies a salve ointment that should assist in the healing. It's a concoction she learned from her mother many years ago. She never dreamed she would be applying it to a man after being whipped by roman guards. "Okay, that will have to do. You can sleep here on this bed. I will be in the next room. You have a strange manner about you, but there is something familiar about you. Please try to be as quiet as possible. That will make it easier for you to blend in. My neighbors are understanding to a point. We don't want them to have to choose between your freedom or theirs. Hopefully, our friends will arrive tomorrow, and we can travel. Good night."

David nods in an assuring way, "Yes, and thank you for everything you've done for me today."

CHAPTER 6

A FACE OF GOD

"Blessed are the pure in heart, for they will see God" Matthew 5:8 NIV

The next morning Mary is preparing a simple breakfast of eggs and bread. David awakens and smells the food cooking and is overwhelmed by how hungry he is since he hasn't eaten in over 24 hours. He struggles to sit up and then reaches for the wall to assist in his standing up. The pain in his back is intense, but he is comforted by the fact that the wounds are now on the mend. He limps slowly in to the next room where Mary stands working on the food. David sits down at a simple table careful not to let his back touch anything. David says, "Good Morning! I can't say that was the most comfortable night's sleep I've had, but it certainly beats trying to sleep in prison with six snoring cell mates. I'm not used to sleeping on my stomach all night, but whenever I tried to roll over, my wounds reminded me I was happy right where I was."

Mary chastises David, "You make a joke over something that was very serious and very dangerous. You managed to get yourself flogged and thrown in prison after only one day in our city. Now we have to be very careful when we move about because it will not go unnoticed that you have escaped from prison. If you are caught, they will do more than whip you. I assure you, if caught, they will interrogate us about Jesus then execute both of us for my part in this."

David feeling admonished replies, "I'm sorry, and please believe me when I say how thankful I am that you rescued me from that prison and those guards. I am forever in your debt. You're right, though. When I think of last night, that truly was a miracle springing me from that horrible place." David takes a deep smell and asks, "What are you making? It smells delicious!"

Mary answers, "I have some milk, a couple eggs I am scrambling, and some bread warming. It is not much, but you are welcome to all that I have."

"That sounds wonderful. I am famished," David replied.

Mary has looked through the drawing package more out of curiosity. She tells David, "I hope you don't mind, but I looked at your drawings. They are very good. I don't understand all of them, but the ones of the young girl are incredible. Who is she?"

David smiles, "That is totally fine. Thank you. She is my daughter, Patty. She will be fourteen years old very soon, and I promised her to draw a picture of her for her birthday."

Mary smiles, "She is a very beautiful young girl."

David is curious about Mary and her life. He asks, "Thank you. I think she is beautiful too. So, do you live here by yourself, or do you have a husband?"

Mary hesitates a moment to answer. She doesn't usually get asked about her personal life especially by a total stranger. She knows this is a slightly different situation, and she doesn't want to offend David. She thinks about how she will answer his question, "No, I live by myself. No man would be allowed to have me because of my past life. But, I have given up that life, and am more blessed than I could ever have hoped or imagined."

Mary finishes preparing the food and places two servings on the table. She sits down across from them and before eating she bows her head and says a simple prayer. David prays silently along with her and then looks up. Mary nods and they begin their meal. David takes a drink of the milk and almost coughs all of it up. Some of it comes out of his nose and he apologizes as he wipes his face. He says, "the milk taste caught me by surprise. What kind is it?"

Mary responds, "goat milk."

"It's interesting. I have never tasted goat milk before."

Mary just shrugs and wonders what person would never have had goat milk in their life. More strangeness.

Again, David has a strange feeling come over him. Could this actually be Mary Magdalene whom Jesus spared from being stoned because she was a prostitute? She was dragged before Jesus by the religious leaders, and they asked Him what should be done with a woman who had sinned against God. Jesus answered them and said by all means she should be stoned to death, but let the first person without sin cast the first stone. Thwarted by Jesus' logic Mary was set free, and Jesus told her to sin no more. Now, here she was a disciple of his, and able to live her life free. David wondered about his journey here beginning with dreaming of this woman across space and time.

They initially ate their breakfast in silence. Both were still exhausted from the trauma from the previous day. The eggs and bread tasted so good to David. He even managed to drink the milk after he got used to the taste. He could easily have eaten three times the amount of food she prepared. But, he was grateful for the meal and let her know. "This is delicious Mary. Thank you for sharing your food with me."

Mary nodded her approval, "I was wondering about something you said last night, and hoped you wouldn't mind me asking."

David shook his head, "no not at all. What did I say that has you wondering?"

Mary replied, "You said I was a figment of your imagination that you had dreamt about for a month? What did you mean by that?"

David thinks about this for a moment and considers the best way to answer. David hesitates and then says, "Mary, I'm from a place very very far from here. All of your ways are very different than where I am from." He decided to stay away from the 'I am from the future' concept because that might confuse or really scare her. "Somehow, I have been brought here in a most bizarre way. Everything that is unfolding has a purpose, and now I know it is God's plan. Meeting you, and hopefully meeting Jesus in the near future is beyond my full comprehension, but I am doing my best to embrace it. However, I will tell you I am excited by the possibility."

Mary smiles, "Thank you, that helps me learning more about you as well."

David wants to go into more detail about Mary and her story, but a knock on the door interrupts their conversation. They both look at each other with fear, but a familiar voice to

Mary speaks up through the door, "Mary, it's us. Please let us in!"

Mary breathes a sigh of relief tells David to wait there and rushes to the other room to open the door, "Thank goodness it's you! We hoped you would get here so we could get moving. I'm fearful of a search by the Romans."

Three men walk inside and they shut the door behind. The first man says, "Thank goodness, you are okay. We feared the worst when we passed the prison this morning. We heard shouting, a lot of doors slamming and many centurions scattering. They have been rounding up people to question them."

Mary takes a deep breath. It's one thing to offer yourself as a sacrifice, quite another to actually risk it all. She replies, "I found the man just where our Lord said I would. All the guards and prisoners were asleep. The doors opened without any effort, even the cell door. We walked out of the prison without alarming anyone. We nearly ran into a centurion guard when we got outside, and I knew we were caught, but he looked past us in the dark and then continued on. My heart raced so hard, I was sure he could hear my heart beating within my chest. I witnessed another of his many miracles. This man, David, is different. He speaks about strange things, and yet, there is something familiar about him. He even says he has seen me in his dreams. I can only imagine what is in store for him."

The second man says, "I still don't understand why the master would take such a risk with your life for a complete stranger. The risks to you and all of us are far too great! Is he ready to move?"

Mary responds, "The Romans did a thorough job on him with their whip. Fortunately, he does not appear to have any broken bones, and should be able to travel."

The third man says, "Our master wants us to bring him right away. The Romans will be expanding their search radius this morning. We need to leave as soon as possible."

She turns to David who has approached Mary and the three men, "David, these men are also disciples of Jesus, let me introduce you to…"

David interrupts her, "No, please let me guess!" They all look strangely at David. He looks at the first man, "Judging by your direct manner, I would guess you are Matthew who was once a tax collector." Matthew has a shocked look on his face. He says to Mary, "Did you tell him about us?"

Mary replies, "No, but I told you there is a strangeness about this man!"

David gives them a shrug and continues to the second man, "And you have to be my favorite disciple… Peter who was once Simon, and a pretty good fisherman."

Peter is slightly shocked by David's guess, "How could you possibly know this? I've never met you before in my life."

David now faces the third man, but cannot guess with any certainty who he might be. He says, "Hello, I don't have a guess for you. My name is David Campbell, and I am pleased to meet you."

The third man replies, "Hello, my name is Judas Iscariot."

David is instantly shocked and repulsed by this revelation. He takes a step back and gives a strange almost angry look. Judas cannot understand the "cold" response from David. Matthew and Peter give strange looks because of David's reaction to their brother disciple.

Peter lightens up the mood, "Hah, Judas, I see you have the same effect on strangers as you have on us!" Peter turns toward David and in a more serious tone, "What is the matter with you? We have travelled a great distance to fetch you. These are extremely perilous times, yet you treat one of our own with such disrespect?" David regains his composure and sets his 'feelings' aside for the moment. He reaches out again and shakes Judas' hand and then the other two disciples. He says, "It was nothing. I am very sorry. It is an honor to meet all of you. It's just that I am in a state of absolute amazement and confusion all at the same time. Meeting all of you here is almost beyond comprehension. Please excuse any bad behavior on my part. Trust me, you all mean so much to me!"

Judas warms to David's explanation and states, "Well then, let me be the first of us to welcome you. Our Master has sent us on this journey explicitly to fetch you back to him. I understand the romans treated you very poorly. Are you able to travel?"

Matthew adds, "Yes, will we have to also carry you on our backs?"

Judas admonishes Matthew, "Matthew, please be courteous, or at least be quiet."

David is taking all this talk in and wonders at the dynamics between the three disciples. He answers, "I can travel. Believe me, to meet Jesus, I would walk to the ends of the world!" Mary gives David a look at this remark. Her curiosity about David is almost overwhelming, but she holds her tongue and knows that she will learn what she needs to learn in time. Right now they need to get ready for their trip.

Matthew says, "Pack up your things and let us get moving! We must move fast, but not do anything to attract attention from the Romans. They are going to definitely be on alert for you."

The five people: three disciples, one woman, and David head outside to begin their journey. They are walking at a slightly hurried pace. David is struggling inside to keep up, but doesn't want the others to know. So, with every step he has to put effort into not limping and not letting his back pain show. At one point early on they pass another roman centurion, and David, not realizing what he is doing, gives him a long stare.

The centurion realizing this person before him is staring says, "What are you **staring** at, Hebrew? Do you need a few lashes from my whip to straighten your eyes?"

Mary steps between and addresses the centurion, "No, centurion. Our apologies. He is not feeling well as you can see from his bandages. He received a bad blow to his head in a fall. He is a bit dazed."

The centurion abruptly and unexpectedly turns and walks away. Mary glares at David and grabs David by the arm and gives him a firm tug. David winces in pain realizing it was his dislocated arm. He whispers to her, "I'm sorry!"

Mary walks over to Matthew and says, "Did you see that? The centurion just turned and walked away! I thought we were dead for sure!" She turns back to David, "What are you trying to do? Get all us beaten and thrown back into jail, or worse? Do not do anything to antagonize these men."

David replies, "I'm not trying to do anything! Everything here is strange to me. It's hard to not look around and wonder about everything." It was true. Every sound, smell and sight were a wonder to David. The experience was almost overwhelming to his senses. No book, story or movie of this time period had prepared him for the actualities surrounding him now. Everything was mesmerizing.

Mary shakes her head at him, "Please keep walking and try not to draw attention to us. These men need no excuse to pull us aside, and when they find out who we are, our fates will be sealed."

Peter raises his voice at both of them, "Stop it, both of you! We have several miles to travel today. Is it necessary for you to argue the entire way?"

"I'm not arguing," replied Mary, "I'm simply trying to keep our new found friend here from getting us all thrown into prison!"

Matthew chimes in, "He's not my friend. I cannot for the life of me understand why our master risked your life, and sent us all this way to find this man and bring him back with us! We risk everything, and for what? To aid a complete stranger?"

Peter responds, "Matthew, my blunt friend, you certainly have a way with people. The master does not need to explain to you, or any of us, what he intends for this man. He wasn't even here, and yet he instructed each of us to go to Mary's house. He told us exactly what we would find! It happened exactly as he said it would. He even told me in private the stranger would already know us! When we arrived he guessed each of names after only hear us talk for a few minutes! How can you doubt his words or have not have faith in him sending us to do his bidding? It matters not for a friend or a complete stranger, his will be done and without question."

Judas says, "he didn't know me, but I get your point!"

Mary adds, "Yes Matthew, you be nice, or I'll tell the master how you mistreated his disciple!"

This revelation shocks David, "Mary, how did you know I am a disciple of Jesus?"

Mary thinks for a second and says, "I saw it in your eyes when I first said his name to you. It was like you awoke from a dream and realized your true surroundings. You seem to be on a journey of your own which I don't completely understand, but I believe you are here at his will, and he makes disciples out of some very interesting people. Present company included!"

David is enthralled at Mary's explanation. He smiles at her, "Thank you. When you say it out loud, it was exactly like that. This is really quite amazing! I am in awe at the thought of walking in this land at this time on our way to meet Jesus."

Peter is listening to this back and forth discussion between Mary and David. It is really a strange undertaking, and this new person is different somehow, but he seems genuine in his desire to meet Jesus. It's more than desire. There is love in his voice when he refers to Jesus. Peter says, "Well that depends on whether I can get this group moving in the same direction. Now let's go before the Romans think we're planning an uprising to overthrow them, and haul us off in chains to prison." With that, the caravan of five pick up their pace and head off towards their destination.

The centurion had walked off for several yards when he stopped, shook his head and looked around. He was a bit confused. Another centurion approached him and asked,

"Why did you walk away from that group of people? Are you sure they weren't with the man we are seeking?"

The first centurion replied, "I do not think so. I was questioning the man and then a woman interrupted us. I am sure he is not the one we are searching for, but I cannot explain why."

"That whole group," continued the second centurion, "seemed suspicious to me. I heard them mention Jesus' name. There is much interest in this man especially amongst the Jewish leadership. We must report this to the captain of the guards immediately. Did you see which direction they were headed in?"

The first centurion shook his head and said, "No! I turned and looked in the direction they were heading, and they disappeared in a flash. Very strange."

The centurions begin a quick search in the general area, but to no avail. The curious group of strangers have disappeared and are nowhere to be found. They widen their search area and question several people, but without any additional luck. They hope the captain of the guards will not hold them personally responsible for losing a group of five suspicious Hebrews. They are all nervous because of the breach of security the night before at the prison. The guard in charge of the cells has been severely reprimanded and beaten because of the careless loss of the man and his possessions. The captain had wanted a detailed explanation of the man and was agitated at the apparent lack of security. The guard's replacement will be a lot more careful, or suffer a similar fate.

Not too far off, two centurions have traced the strange man's origins back to Joshua's carpentry shop. Both Joshua and Rebecca are brought to the captain as part of the ongoing investigation.

Captain Aurelius looks up from his notes and says, "Since security is my primary concern for this city, I put a strong emphasis on tracking all strange activities. It took us a while to find you, and link you to the man who escaped from our prison. Now, tell me everything you know about this man."

Both Joshua and Rebecca are nervous to have been brought before the captain. They know by reputation the man can be cruel especially to the Hebrew populace. Many people have disappeared into the Roman prisons never to be heard from again. Joshua clears his throat and answers a bit nervously, "I don't know captain. As I stated earlier, he crashed through the roof of my carpentry shop. I don't know how he got on my roof in the first place. He hurt his head and shoulder in the accident. My wife bandaged his head and shoulder, and then he left."

The captain continued, "Just like that. He didn't say, or do anything to give you any clue to his identity? I'm warning you. If you withhold information, no matter how small, it will not sit well with the Prefect. It is my sworn duty to protect this land for the Prefect and King Herod."

Rebecca looked at Joshua and tried to remember the strange things David had spoken about while he was with them. She finally said, "His name was David. He spoke of strange things and places I did not understand. He was going to hail a TAX-I, and go to his King David HO-TELL. We didn't know what to make of him. He was insistent on leaving, but we don't know where he was going and he never told us where he was from."

Joshua takes the cue from his wife and continues, "But, as you can see, he spoke such strange things. Perhaps he was possessed. Or, simply out of his mind from the wound to his head. But, I am confused. How could he have possibly escaped from your prison?"

Captain Aurelius rises from his chair, nostrils flaring, angrily he commands, "Centurion! Take this pair of Hebrews to the town square and give them five lashes each. That will teach them a lesson about keeping secrets from the Roman Empire, and questioning our ability to control them. And find that prisoner! I want this city turned upside down until he is found!"

David is walking along side Peter and asks, "Peter I'm curious. Do you mind if I ask you how long have you been serving your master?"

"Almost two years now," Peter replies. He thinks a moment before continuing, "He told me to put down my nets and I would fish for men! It has not been an easy transition from fishing to being his disciple. But, I have seen many things that show me Jesus is the Messiah that our nation has waited for a very long time. But he has come in a very different way than I expected. When I was young, I was taught by my rabbis the scripture predicted the messiah would come as a mighty king to save the nation of Israel from those would seek to destroy us or enslave us. But, Jesus doesn't confront the Romans, or build up an army. His message is to love one another without hesitation, to even love those who would do us wrong. He teaches us to reach out to the least desirable among us with a message of hope. He performs miracles that prove he is a man sent from God. He even goes against the religious leadership of our tribe trying to get them to understand the things he has come to teach all of us. I am not able to grasp and understand all the things he has said and done. He says his time is not yet at hand, and all things will be revealed to each of us. I have come to believe he is the Messiah of prophesy, and have a faith that will endure."

David is almost leaping as he hears Peter's description of their ministry. David blurts out, "I believe the scriptures predicted exactly what you have experienced, and there is so much more to come!"

Matthew has been listening to their conversation and is struck by David's response. He asks, "How can you know of such things or predict the future of our ministry?"

David tries to speak an answer, but the words are stuck in his mouth. Matthew mutters a guttural "hmph" almost saying 'just as I thought.' Finally David manages, "I cannot say and perhaps you are right. How much farther to our destination?"

Peter replies, "It's not far now. How is your body holding up? We will need to keep a close eye on your wounds. We don't want them to fester."

David's back aches with every step, but his anticipation keeps the pain in check. He doesn't want to sound too excited about the prospect of meeting Jesus, but he cannot fathom a more profound experience. He decides to be honest, "I am in a lot of pain, but I don't want to stop."

They press on and get to the place where they are camping out. They have a fire going. There are only two additional people there. David is introduced to James and John. David looks around anxiously for Jesus, but he is nowhere to be found. He finally asks, "Where is Jesus? I am very anxious to meet him."

James replies, "my brother has gone off to meditate and pray before dinner. He has told us to expect a guest and to welcome you as one of our own. So, welcome my friend! David, tell us, where do you come from?"

David smirks and holds back a tear at the thought of his wife and daughter. "You would not believe me if I told you. Suffice it to say that I come from a place very very far from here."

Judas is now more curious about this strange man and asks, "What do you do in the faraway place to make a living?"

David answers, "Well... I am the senior pastor of a Christian church. A pastor is like a rabbi."

The word 'Christian' is lost on the group and they give David a strange look. Judas continues, "What kind of church is a Christian Church?"

David stumbles a bit at this question, but takes a breath and forges ahead, "it is a holy building dedicated to teaching the Gospel of Jesus Christ. I'm not sure how else to explain it to you."

A man from behind David approaches and says, "You should not be afraid to answer these questions. We have travelled to many places and all of these men and women have seen miracles performed in the name of my father in heaven. You also preach the good news about my father. Hello, I am Jesus. I have called you to this place... and time. Please come walk with me."

Jesus reaches out with his hand and grabs David's hand and helps him to his feet. A wave of energy flows through David at Jesus' touch. David realizes Jesus has lifted him up to his feet pulling on the dislocated arm! A moment ago, it was extremely painful to lift or rotate his arm, but now all the pain is gone! David slowly reaches around to his back, and strokes it where the centurion had left him with deep wounds. He can feel the streaks where scar tissue has formed, but there is no pain to the touch there either! He reaches up and realizes his head wound is gone and only a small scar and bump remain. He removes the wrapping expecting some blood to be on his fingers from touching the wound. Nothing, and the wound has no pain to the touch. It feels completely healed. David is stunned to silence which he did not expect. Jesus smiles at him in understanding. They walk several yards continuing in silence. Finally, Jesus stops and turns to David, smiles and says, "David, you look like a man with a question or two!"

David shakes his head a bit more frantically than he would have liked in this situation, and answers, "more like a million questions, my Lord... But can I start with, are you really my Lord, Jesus Christ? The Messiah and the Son of God?"

Jesus states, "Yes, I am Jesus of Nazareth. The world at this time has no notion of the 'Son of God' as you speak for the fullness of my ministry has not been completed. But, doubt not who is standing before you in the flesh. Most people in this time cannot understand how someone with such a humble beginning could be their long-awaited Messiah. I was brought here to be a light to the world for anyone willing to open their eyes, to see and to believe."

"Okay wow, so much for question number one. It is such an honor to be here with you, but how is it I can understand you, and the rest of your disciples? Shouldn't you be speaking in ancient Greek or Hebrew?"

Jesus begins to laugh out loud, and David is taken off guard by this. If there is one image of Jesus he has never considered, it is one of Jesus laughing out loud. David asks, "My Lord, why are you laughing? What could possibly be so funny?"

Jesus stops laughing, "Your question struck me as very funny, so I laughed. Don't you find it even slightly humorous to be standing here with me, dressed as you are, having travelled this far through time and asking me how you can understand me? Language and understanding should never be a problem amongst people who truly wish to know and understand each other and seek the truth. When two people, or twenty people want to communicate, they shed their differences and speak as in a community. Open communication can bridge any gap when both sides come to the table willing to listen and have respect for the other side of the table. It saddens me when people speak their minds without the intention of hearing the other side to an issue. Especially when their minds are filled with anger, spite, or worse, hatred for another man's beliefs and ideals." Jesus pauses for this to sink in with David. "What else?"

"That is profound, and every person should apply that to their daily lives. To be quite honest, I'm still trying to find the humor in all of this. But, okay," David continues, "next question. How did I get here to this place and this time? Why have you chosen me with this... this... I'm not really sure how to phrase it: this epic adventure?"

Jesus replies, "If you truly believe who I say I am, then the answer to your question should be self-evident. Time has no limit to my father in heaven. He knows all from the beginning of time to the end. All things are possible to those who believe in him, and have complete trust. To the second part of your question, when a good servant strays from his master's side, should the master simply find a new servant, or should he bring the good servant back to his side, and help to resolve the problems that led him astray? Do you not remember the parable of the lost sheep where the shepherd left the 99 to recover the one? The shepherd risked the entire flock because of his concern for his one lost sheep!"

Slightly hurt, David asks, "Do you believe that I have strayed from your flock Lord?"

"A person's path is always shifting and changing." Jesus continues, "Sometimes the path is easy and so a man says, 'This path is too easy, I must seek a more difficult path, and I will do more good on this new path.' When the path turns uphill with many stones and obstacles to block the way, the man says, 'This path strains me to my soul. I must cross over and walk a different path.' Each person struggles with the paths of their life. Each struggle tests us, and the bigger the stones, the harder the struggle. We must choose how we want to navigate our paths. We can go left, go right, go over, go under, go back, or stand still with regard to the obstacle. What matters most is the choices we make as we push past each stone in our lives. Each choice can be correct. Even standing still can be the right choice while we wait for an answer to present itself. If you seek peace and joy in the midst of the struggle with the choices you make, you will live a happier life and the choices you make will give you a deeper satisfaction. No man has walked the same path for his entire life!"

David blurts out, "but you have my Lord! You walked a perfect path for your entire life! That's what I believe at the core of my being."

Jesus nods his assent, "My path is truly unique as is each person's and it is a very difficult one to be sure. At every turn in the road, I try to meet each stone I encounter with the knowledge that choosing peace and joy will result in a happier outcome. I choose to fulfill my father's wishes even unto the very end of the age." Jesus stops and reaches for David's drawings. He looks them over and stops on the one of David's daughter. "This 'special encounter'... this gift my father has bestowed on you will ultimately glorify him because your journey will be clear for the rest of your life. This gift will not remove the stones from your path, or make your paths easier, but it will give you the resolve to grow in your faith each time you face a new obstacle in your path. You seek clarity and a renewed purpose for your life, and that is exactly what my father has chosen to give you. The ripples that emanate from your teaching will have profound effects on many souls who find my father through you. Each new soul sends out their ripples and they will compound unto eternity. This is the ultimate reason why you are here to be restored, and to give you a clear vision of your mission."

David is a bit humbled, "Why me Lord? I don't feel worthy of this gift especially given my recent struggles."

Jesus reaches over and puts a hand on David's shoulder to reassure him, "Throughout man's history, my father has chosen very special discreet moments in time to intervene directly in the lives of his children. You are one of these moments in time. As you move forward, the lives you touch and the people you save will have an eternal purpose. My hope is you will encourage your flock to grow deeper in their faith, and walk with that faith each and every day!"

David's body shudders and he begins to weep, "Thank you Lord! I will!" David thinks about his life choices and asks, "Are we free to make all of our choices in our lives, or are they somehow already mapped out and chosen for us?"

"That is the beauty of world," Jesus replies, "Every person chooses the life they live. A person stands at a crossroads, and asks, 'Should I go left, or should I go right?' Their choice is as free as the bird flying overhead. My father knows all the choices of all the days of their lives before they are born. Some choices make him sad, but most make him proud of his children. To be sure, each person chooses freely and must live with the consequences of each choice."

David wonders, "Lord, when will you return to the world again?"

Jesus says, "for those who believe, I have already come! Because of their faith, they have secured a home in my father's kingdom. For all the days of their lives, they can live securely knowing a heavenly home awaits them. For those who do not believe, I will come as a thief in the night, stealing their most prized possessions. My life is given for all and until all of mankind has heard my father's word, I remain as only a hope to the world. My spirit will continue to roam freely in and amongst believers and non-believers. But oh the joy in my father's heart when someone chooses to believe."

Jesus returns his gaze to the picture of Patty, "The children of the world will forever be our hope for the future. You have a beautiful daughter. Your skill and artistry are magnificent, however, you should complete your work."

David regains his composure. This statement strikes him as an odd thing to say. A bit confused he states, "I thought it was completed."

Jesus continues, "It hasn't been signed by the artist who created it. Are you ashamed of what you have created?"

David thinks about this and replies, "No Lord! I have always felt it would be a prideful act on my behalf to sign my drawings since my gift comes from… well, you!"

"Without your signature," Jesus responds, "how will people who see your beautiful work know you are proud of the gift my father has given you? Every drawing you make is an acknowledgement to the world of the gift freely given to you from my father in heaven. Your signature announces it to the world! Each of us are blessed with gifts and talents to use for God's kingdom. Examine your heart whenever you are unsure whether an act or thought is a sin. If it pleases, honors or praises the Lord, then it is not a sin. If it is done out of love or respect, then it is not a sin. Pride, deceit, deception and other trappings bring man to their lowest points and give sin a stronghold in their lives. Their purpose becomes entangled in it, and it can be all consuming. Resist and repent when you come to realize the sinful nature of your ways. Only then can you be a true child of God." Jesus hands the drawing back to David and turns to leave. "I will spend the rest of the day alone in meditation and prayer. We will talk more tomorrow when you have had a chance to think of more questions."

David thinks to himself, 'that should not be a problem' and he bows as Jesus passes him. David stands there for a moment not really knowing what to do. This encounter has been monumentally epic. Off in the distance, Jesus pauses he turns his head slightly and he hears Jesus say, "perhaps it would be good for you to also meditate on everything that has transpired! Nothing would please your father more..."

The next morning David is sitting next to the fire with the other disciples. Judas has put a cup of water in a precarious spot above Peter's head as he sleeps. When Peter moves, the cup spills on him and he jumps up and looks around for the perpetrator of the practical joke. Peter is angry initially, but everyone around him is laughing and pointing at Judas as the instigator. Peter begins to laugh as well.

Judas laughingly says, "It is a true sign of character when a man can laugh at himself."

"Judas, my brother," Peter replies, "I'm not laughing at myself. I am only laughing at the thought of the revenge I will take out on you when you least expect it! You should consider sleeping with one eye open tonight!" This brings about another round of laughter. David is sitting with his drawings and is amazed at the group of men surrounding him. They relate to one another with such ease even though they live a rugged and dangerous life. The discussions between the disciples from the night before ranged from a mixture of worry over where they will be traveling next, to the general state of their land being occupied and controlled at the hands of the Romans. He even caught a few discussions and glances about him and the nature off his visit, and the strangeness of his arrival. It made David a bit self-conscious, but he knows his purpose for being here was clear. He does want to connect more closely with these men. They are living a unique life and he wants to fully experience as much of it as possible. James walks over and asks David if he can look at his drawings. He nods and James peers at them. James says, "David, these drawings are quite remarkable. How long have you been creating such works of art?"

"Thank you, James. I have been drawing for many years. Since I was a young boy. It's something that gives me great joy and peace." He says these words and reflects back on what Jesus had said to him about seeking peace and joy, and realizes they coincided exactly with how he reacts to the stones in his path of life. "If you see a drawing you like, please feel free to keep it as a gift."

James asks, "What are you drawing now?"

"Actually, with your permission, I would like to draw you and the other disciples as you go about your day," David replies.

"I would be honored! Do you want me to pose, sit still or can you draw me as we move about? As you've seen, we can be quite raucous and playful with one another. However, please don't believe we are not working hard. It is nice to relax our ways and unwind a bit when we are amongst our most trusted. Most days we are teaching the crowds and trying to help our master spread the good news about God. It's difficult because most people lose hope in these times. When Jesus speaks to them, a light goes on inside many and they believe God is with him. He gives people hope where most only held despair."

David replies, "Thank you. I know you live in difficult times, and I really appreciate all the work you do to spread God's word. Just keep doing what you would normally do. I prefer to draw you at work." James returns the drawings to

David, and goes over and sits down next to Matthew. David sketches the two men talking and engaging. They have strong stark features. Their hands are rough and calloused from their hard lives. Their faces are weathered and their beards are a bit unkempt. Everyone is wearing similar long flowing robes with head pieces. The two men wave their hands and arms about expressively as each tries to make or emphasize his own point of view. As David draws, he listens to the conversation and the tone of their speech. They both have an easiness and surety of where they are, and what they are doing. He remembers his last conversation with Bill and how much stress he felt in that meeting. More than that, though David realizes, the last six months have lacked the friendly easiness between him and his entire church staff. Conversations and meetings have been strained with counting how many people walk through their doors each week; Where the money will come from for their recently planned capital campaign and church expansion; So much work to be done and never having enough resources to handle each ministry. It has put a level of stress on everyone, and the way they have been handling it, has not been very... well.. Godly. Watching these men interact this way in this tough environment with everything they have to do even just to survive on a daily basis leaves David with a sense of a longing to return to a simpler existence, or at least to start to appreciate everything he has in his life. He is filled with an emptiness for his family whom he misses dearly. He wonders if he will ever see them again. Jesus had said David's message for the rest of his life would be clear, but he didn't say from where... or when! He can only hope that this dream or reality will somehow bring him back to his family and friends.

David completes the drawing of Peter and Matthew. He has captured them in their natural state with their expressive natures. Peter has his hand outstretched almost pointing, and Matthew has his arm juxtaposed allowing the person seeing this picture to think they are debating with opposite opinions. Their faces are stern, but not angry.

David starts on another drawing of Mary sitting with Judas. Judas has a seriousness about him, but even he is casual in his dealings with Mary and the other disciples. The joke he played on Peter earlier was completely unexpected. David cannot explain to them why he feels what he feels without complicating his situation. Mary smiles from beneath her frock and head covering. She is listening to Judas with intensity, but she shakes her head 'no' a few times telling him she disagrees with his point of view. David draws Judas with his hand resting on Mary's shoulder, and the other arm partially extending toward her with his index finger pointing beyond her. Judas is wondering about the details of her experience in the prison. So, he asks her to fill him in on all the details or their adventure. She hesitates a couple times and has to catch her breath because the event was so intense, but exhilarating at the same time. Looking back Mary realizes there were many parts to the night at the prison; each one miraculous in its own way. Mary says, "The guard at the entrance was nowhere to be found, so I just walked into the building. Normally, the entrance would have been locked and required a key to gain entrance, but this door and the other doors I encountered not only were unlocked, but were all slightly ajar. Even the cell door where David was located was open just slightly. The guard in the outer room was sound asleep at his table. The prisoners were also asleep. The only person awake in the entire building besides me was David. It was an eerie feeling, but it matched what Jesus told me would occur exactly. We retreated and kept as silent as possible until we reached my house. At one point a centurion guard came within a few feet of us. I thought he would discover the two of us for sure, but he passed right by us. I have never been more scared in all my life!"

"Yes," Judas adds, "that was quite an exhilarating experience. The implications of being caught would have been horrific. I'm not sure the request was worth the risk." Mary shakes her head, "No! That's exactly my point! As scary as it was, I don't think there was any true danger involved because we were under God's guidance and protection." Judas starts to disagree, but changes his mind and says, "Well, I'm happy for the outcome and your safety."

David is finishing the second drawing of Judas and Mary. He looks up to see Jesus approaching him. Jesus comes over and sits down next to David. He nods approvingly at the drawing. He picks up the other drawing just completed and is joined by all the disciples.

Judas remarks, "David, these drawings are fantastic. And you completed them in a relatively short amount of time. Your talent is undeniable. Am I truly this handsome?" Matthew punches Judas on the shoulder, "your pride will be your undoing!"

"Thank you Judas, and yes you are. It would not be honest for me to draw you any other way," David replies.

Jesus pulls David a couple feet aside and asks, "Tell me David, what is "The Good News" you preach to people when you are home?" David is a bit nervous at this question not because of the answer, but because he is fearful of revealing too much to the other people around them. Jesus senses his hesitation, "you needn't fear revealing all that you know. You are but a whisper in time here. After you are gone, nobody will be able to recall the details of your visit. It is how my Father has designed it. He wanted you to experience this life, and believe in me by allowing you to see and feel everything first hand in the world that I live in. Everything you see and hear is as real to you as it is to those around you, but for obvious reasons, our two worlds cannot collide. The reality would be too harsh and quite unbelievable for the others. So, you are free to speak your mind, I ask again, what do you preach to the people in your church?"

David is so relieved at hearing this explanation for two reasons. It saves him from having to worry about saying anything that would alter the future, and it gives him hope of returning home. He says, "That Jesus Christ was born of his mother the virgin Mary. He lived a perfect sinless life, was betrayed into the hands of sinners by one of his own disciples. He was put to death on the cross, buried, but after three days was resurrected, just as he claimed he would. After a time, he ascended into heaven to sit on the thrown of heaven at his Father's right hand! He did all of this to save the world from sin because mankind could not hope to save themselves."

Jesus nods and affirms what David is saying and then asks, "Why do you wish to stop preaching this message? What would you have become of your life? Your gift of preaching is profound and is a great gift from my father."

David lowers his head a bit in shame, "I found myself judging and condemning the people I was preaching to for their lack of concern for the world. We have so many poor and homeless, but my congregation seemed oblivious to the ills of the world. They live with so much wealth and affluence. They separate themselves from people with less. With all our efforts, it seems the world is getting worse, not better. I have become bitter, and have started to feel that I cannot make a difference, or make even the slightest dent in the problems of the world. Even in my local community there are poor and defenseless people who live lives in such destitute conditions. My heart is especially torn for the children caught up in these circumstances because they didn't do anything to deserve their plights. These people are desperate for help, and yet I feel powerless to come to their aid."

"You will always have the poor," Jesus answers, "and your mission should continue to help them as much as possible. Each person is on a journey through life. They choose their path, and must live their life according to the choices they make. That is how my Father designed the world. It is wrong for you to condemn your congregation for **your** lack of faith."

David is chagrined at this charge from Jesus, and he fires back, "Lord? My lack of faith? I did not think my feelings were the stirrings of a lack of faith in you. I have dedicated my life to teaching your word."

"It is faith that holds you to your path," replied Jesus. "A crowd gathered at the base of a large rock, and waited, for they had heard the rock could deliver wisdom and truth to all who listened. But the rock remained silent, and the crowd went away without wisdom or truth touching their hearts. How is my church to grow and believe without my message being delivered by you? How will people hear wisdom and discern truth from my rock if you remain silent?"

David nods his understanding and says, "But, I assure you, there is no lack of faith now!"

Jesus says, "You are the recipient of a wonderful gift and have witnessed me yourself first hand. You are blessed and favored by my father. How much more I will bless those who believe in me without seeing. But they must be taught about God through his word to understand the truth and the way to the kingdom of heaven."

David is still stinging from Jesus' accusation. He asks in a lowered voice, "Is that why you brought me here Lord?"

"No," Jesus replies, "That is just one of the many reasons my father has chosen to bring you here to this place and time. He wanted you to experience the full measure of what it is to be a disciple of Jesus living in the time of King Herod. He wanted you to meet other disciples, and truly understand what it is to be poor of money and possessions, but rich in spirit, devotion, kindness and most of all love. Soon, you must return home and continue your teaching. I agree... you'll have renewed vigor now when you stand before your own flock! Maybe you can ask Judas to give you some good practical jokes to play on your staff just to lighten everyone's mood. But they may need to be translated to your time, no?" At this last statement Jesus burst out into laughter.

David just stares at him in amazement. He finally says, "I love your laugh, Lord. In all my years of scripture study, I've never envisioned you laughing, or being amused. In scripture you deliver these serious messages, parables and sermons. Sometimes, I can sense contentment in your teaching when you speak of love or caring for children, but I have never thought of you as laughing out loud at a joke or a funny statement. The pure enjoyment of life in your manner has been awe inspiring."

Jesus replies, "Thank you. It is a rare person in these times, or any time for that matter, who can laugh without holding back. When you stop and think about it, in your lifetime, which moments were your happiest? When we are children, laughter is as easy as waking up. As we grow older we take ourselves much too seriously. I lived a whole life before this one as a child and a young adult. My ministry didn't start until I was almost thirty years old. Despite the hardships growing up, there was love and laughter in my home with my mother, father and brothers. It's the best way to live your life. Laugh, David, at every chance God gives you, laugh. Don't hold back the goodness of laughter."

"I find myself happiest when I am consumed with a new drawing, or spending time with my wife and daughter," David replies.

"That is just a different kind of laughter from within," Jesus continues, "I've watched while you draw, and your soul is filled with laughter. That is a good thing. You were called to bring light to a desperate world that wishes to hide the truth under a bowl blocking out all light and all hope. Even if you bring the light to a single life, my father is pleased."

"Thank you!" David replies, "You've given me a lot to consider about the future of my ministry and my life." David contemplates everything Jesus has told him. He asks, "I can't help asking myself why I actually like Judas... Considering the despicable role he plays in history. Is he truly the same person who betrays you to the Romans and the pharisees?"

Jesus looks over to where Judas is standing. He says, "All of my disciples have been chosen by my father with specific roles to be carried out to grow my ministry beyond even their expectations. Judas has no notion of the role he is to play at this time. But you can be sure of the history you already know, that I am to be the center of focus. It's really a moment of choice for people to believe in someone who could sacrifice so much for them."

"Lord," David exclaims, "on the day you are betrayed by that man, you are brutally beaten, mercilessly whipped, kicked, mocked and finally crucified on a cross you until you die. The people whom you care deeply for turn their backs on you, and even choose a criminal to be spared over you! It is such a horrible moment in time, and I cannot let this happen? I must stop Judas from his betraying you! If I can talk sense into him, he might change his course."

David starts to turn toward Judas, but Jesus steps in front of him first. He glares at David and shouts, "Stand down now! You have no say in this matter! Just as Satan tempted me and tried to trick me as a serpent, you cannot change this! It's sinful arrogance for you to think you can change the path my father laid out for his son now! It happened over two thousand years before you were born! All of us are destined to play our part so that a greater kingdom can be won."

David is dizzied by Jesus' affront and takes a step back and tries to apologize, "I only wanted to spare you from the hurt and anguish…"

Jesus, a bit softer now, answers him, "David, the path I must walk is as difficult as any can imagine, and beyond as you well know, but it must be walked by me for the sake of all mankind! Of all the people here right now, you have the best understanding and certainly you must realize the necessity of fulfilling not just some scripture from the prophets before me, but each and every prophesy down to the smallest detail. A kingdom awaits for all who believe, and put their faith in me. My sacrifice will open the doors to this kingdom, and I go not of my will, but as my father wills it."

CHAPTER 7

A FACE IN THE EMPIRE

"I am the resurrection and the life. The one who believes in me will live, even though they die; and whoever lives by believing in me will never die. Do you believe this?""

John 11:25-26 NIV

Jesus has returned to the group and motions for David to come sit near him. "The time is almost at hand for you to leave us David. Mary will escort you back to the city of Jerusalem. Your supernatural adventure is coming to an end."

"Jesus, I don't know if I'm ready to return." David hesitates. "Have I learned the everything I need to learn to restart my ministry? I'm worried I will just settle into my old ways after a while and stop being productive. I miss my family, but this feels like family too." David points to all the disciples, "The way you live is hard, but also so refreshing and alive. Each of you has given up everything to bring your individual talents and treasures and do a ministry that literally will change the world. You're doing ministry in a way that is thrilling and extremely fulfilling. Should I not stay longer and be taught this way first hand?"

"No David, you are ready to return. My father's word is the only guide you will ever need for your ministry to thrive. Teach from there and you will always be on the right and truthful path." Jesus continued, "I promise you will not forget this experience. It has already changed you and set you on a new path. However, I must also caution you to be very wary of sharing this extraordinary experience with other people. It will not be easy or advised because people will not be ready to believe what you have experienced. You would be mocked, abandoned and held in contempt by the very people who admire you today. You don't want to spiral onto a very difficult path as soon as you land back on your feet."

David replies, "It is difficult to accept, but I understand."

Jesus stands and calls Mary over to where they are standing. "I want you to escort David back to Jerusalem. You must deliver him to Joshua's home and leave him there. It is imperative you do not stay beyond this time, or attempt to assist him further. David must complete this part of his journey on his own from that point on. Wait at your house until the next morning and then you can travel back here. Please follow these instructions exactly as I have given them to you." She nods her head in understanding. "Now go prepare yourself for the trip back. I will speak some final words to David, and we will meet you back here in two days. Mary walks away and Jesus turns his attention back to David.

"David, I need to explain one final part of your journey. This is very important and I want you to really let my meaning and the implication to you sink in. When you get to Joshua's, your journey home can only be completed by retracing the steps you took to arrive here. You must jump through Joshua's roof at the exact spot you fell through when you first arrived. This action will propel you back home to your time to the same spot you left. As you know many people in the near future here will be persecuted and will martyr themselves in my name and for my sake. It will be a difficult time for Christians. Even today my name is already stirring distrust among the Roman and Jewish leaderships. You have been seen with my disciples and now you are associated with my name and everything that entails. Your trip back to Jerusalem will be perilous as well. You must take great caution in dealing with the threat of capture by the Romans. Your fate for returning safely to your family rests on you and your traveling companion. If you are taken and killed in this time, you perish in your future time as well. Your family will find you in the ruins you fell into without life, and a great tragedy will have occurred. All of the time we have spent together will be for nothing."

David, a bit shaken by this information asks, "isn't there something you can do to protect me from harm? You performed a miracle getting me out of prison. Isn't this just an extension of that assistance?"

Jesus answers, "No, you must have absolute faith in your father in heaven. It is his will that you and I follow. I can only tell you that another person in this time is being blessed with a revelation from my father just as you have been blessed. It will set this person on a path of righteous living and his interactions will set in motion the changes needed for the world. All this is due solely because of you and your interaction with us, but that is all I can say."

Jesus stands as does David who reaches his hand out to shake. Surprisingly, Jesus reaches with both arms and pulls David in for a genuine hug. Jesus whispers, "Bless you from my father above, and thank you for all the lives you have touched and will continue to touch through your ministry."

David is shaking and barely able to respond, "Thank you for your sacrifice!" Jesus looks at him and nods his approval. David feels the emotional weight of what he must do now. He walks toward Mary. She looks up and with a half-smiling half-concerned look on her face starts walking toward him. They have a couple hour hike ahead of them and they should get to the outskirts of Jerusalem by sunset.

"Are you ready to travel? We should get going so we have some light once we arrive."

David replies, "Yes. Give me a moment. I would like to say goodbye to the other men." He walks over to the fire and reaches his hand out to James. "Thank you, brother for your kindness." David then shakes each of the other disciples' hands, and thanks them for welcoming him amongst them.

"David, we are sorry to see you leave so soon. An extra pair of hands in these times is a welcome sight," Judas says.

"I miss my family and friends, but I wish I could continue here with all of you."

"What's the matter? Are your accommodations back in your village not as glamorous as these surroundings?" Judas gives a hearty bellow at the others.

"No, not nearly," David answers. "This is luxury beyond anyone's dream, is it not? And honestly that is part of the special appeal and affection I have for what you are doing."

"Did your meetings with the master give you all the direction you need to accomplish your mission?"

David smiles and says, "You have no idea how much help the master has given me. He is a miracle and a wonder. I will miss seeing you all on a daily basis, but hope you have great success spreading the word of God to the people. I will continue to pray for each of you."

"Be safe and go with God's blessing on you and your family," James replies.

David and Mary start off down the path towards Jerusalem. David pauses to turn and look back at the group of men. They give nods of approval and wave back. David has another wave of emotion about leaving. A monumentally epic encounter, and now he is walking away from the scene of the most significant and sacred person in the history of mankind. How should he feel, he wonders? Then he smiles and says to himself, "Blessed!" David and Mary start up again and disappear from their sight a few hundred yards down the trail.

Mary and David have walked for a while when David starts to whistle a tune. Mary bumps him on the arm and comments, "What is the name of the song you are whistling? It is very beautiful."

David replies, "It's a song from an old movie which just popped into my head a while back called *Climb Every Mountain*. It's from one of my favorite movies of all time, *The Sound of Music*." For a moment David has forgotten his place and only realizes it when he looks at the blank and confused expression on Mary's face. "I'm sorry! Strange and unfamiliar words like *movie* make no sense to you. It's a song I learned a long time ago and it seemed appropriate for our journey. The words to the song go: Climb every mountain, search high and low, follow every highway, every path you know. Climb every mountain, Ford every stream, follow every rainbow, till you find your dream. It's one of mine and my wife's favorite stories. It's about a family who has to find love and survive in troubling times. The music is wonderful."

Mary says, "The words seem to fit our situation. As far as finding love in troubling times, well, that seems to fit my personal situation as well. Thank you for sharing." Mary walks on for a bit. The small road they are traveling is not too difficult, but occasionally it gets a bit rocky. They stop every so often to take a drink of water from a wine skin Mary is carrying. When they pause for a drink she asks, "Tell me about your home. I know you live far off. Do you have a wife and children? I have seen several drawings from your pad. Is this your family?"

"Yes," David replies, "I have a wife and a daughter back home." David pulls Patty's picture from the satchel. "This is my daughter, Patricia. I don't have a sketch of my wife Kathleen, but I sorely miss them both. I cannot wait to return back home to them." David takes the wine skin from Mary and takes a long drink. He hands it back to Mary. "How much farther do you suppose?" It's the same road they took before but David was in such pain and in a more confused state that he lost track of distance and his sense of time.

Every once in a while, they pass other people traveling to or from Jerusalem. They even had to pass by two soldiers who looked them over but didn't trouble them. They are looking for a man with a bandaged head who should barely be able to walk. David has been healed and does not match this description in any way.

David looks at Mary and says, "It's hard not react and stay calm when I see a soldier. It feels like they can see right through to who I am, and know I am the one who escaped from their prison."

Mary says, "You should be safe because they must be looking for a wounded man, as long as we don't run into someone who already knows your face, we should be fine. It won't be much longer, but you have to stay calm and not act differently when we pass by them." David nods his assent. They travel another twenty minutes before they finally get to the town. There are many more guards now, and it is apparent they are on high alert. They are stopped by a guard who asks them where they have been and where they are heading. A moment of panic wells up but David answers, "We have been visiting family, and now we are returning home." The guard gives them the once over. He tells David to remove his head piece. David complies and the guard is satisfied this is not a man who had a severe head trauma only a day ago. The guard grumbly dismisses them and waves then on. David puts his head piece back on, and they quicken their pace away from the soldier. David whispers, "Thank goodness for our master's healing hand." Mary smiles.

As they weave their way through town toward Joshua's house, they reach a point where Mary stops. They are about five houses away from Joshua's and David wonders, "Why have you stopped?"

Mary tries to lift her legs to go further but she physically cannot. She realizes Jesus' words have power and are preventing her from proceeding any further. She says, "I must leave you from here. I wish you a safe journey home, but I can go no further. The house is just ahead on the left. You should recognize it when you get there."

David asks, "Are you sure?"

"I am. I will return back to my house once you leave," Mary responds. "Trust our father in heaven and he will see you through this." David draws close and thanks Mary for everything she has done. "You have been a guiding light for me Mary, the one constant through this whole ordeal. It feels strange to continue on without you, but I will do my best." Mary gives David a hug and whispers in his ear, "Bless you!" Mary turns and heads back in the opposite direction leaving David to consider his next moves. He needs to get to Joshua's house, and then climb onto the roof. The roofs are not high, but he will need help. David looks around and doesn't see anyone. It's just past sunset, but there is still light from the west. As he moves forward, he sees the house. When he gets there, he stops and hesitates before knocking. He didn't leave here on the best of terms. But he will need a boost to get on top of the roof. He sees no other way, and he knocks.

At first there is no response, so he knocks again. Finally, a shuffling sound approaches and the door creaks open. When Joshua realizes who is standing at his threshold, he shouts, "You! I cannot believe you have actually come back here! Why would you do this to me and my family? We have suffered greatly because of you."

David raises and lowers his arm and says, "Please lower your voice Joshua. I only need your help for a moment and I will be out of your life forever."

"Help? Hah," Joshua replies. He turns and exposes his back to David where he has several severe lash wounds from being whipped the day before. "The last time I helped you, this is how I was repaid by our loving overlords. My wife Rebecca suffered much worse, and cannot even get out of bed."

"I'm so sorry, but I had nothing to do with that! I had no idea they did this to you!" David responds. He is not sure why

Joshua would hold him responsible for such a punishment. "Please Joshua, I just need help getting onto your roof. I know that must sound strange, but I assure you that will be the last you see me, ever, I promise."

Joshua shakes his head somewhat violently, "I was barely able to put a small patch up there to block the sun and wind from when you crashed through before. It will be weeks before I am well enough to fix it properly. The last thing in the world I would do is help you back onto my roof! But, I tell you what I will do." Joshua looks around and shouts, "GUARD! GUARD! This is the man you are looking for!" Joshua reaches out and grabs on to David's robe to hold him. Before David realizes it two soldiers come around a nearby corner where they were posted to watch Joshua's neighborhood. David frees himself and starts to run, but they are on him too quickly. They tackle him to the ground and bind his wrists. They hoist David to his feet and David realizes he has fallen into the exact trap Jesus warned him to avoid. He has a sick sinking feeling in his belly and knows he will never get back home to Kathleen and Patty. He lowers his head and begins to weep. The soldiers drag David back to the prison.

When they get to the prison, David fears they will tie him to the whipping post and exact another punishment on him. Knowing full well how much pain eight lashes caused him the other day, David knows he will receive much worse this time! He shudders to think. Surprisingly, they drag him past the whipping post and go directly inside the prison. They take him back to the same cell, open the door and toss him inside without removing the binds on his wrists. The first soldier shakes the door and says, "This time the door is locked for sure. There will be no more mistakes with you!"

David looks up and asks, "where are the other men who were in this cell?" As soon as he asks, he fears the answer.

"They perished one by one by the whip, but feel good because none of them gave up your secret about how you escaped," the second soldier answers. "I'm guessing Captain Aurelius will get that answer out of you directly very shortly." The pit in David's stomach just got a little bit bigger and more sour. He slumps down in the cell and begins to shake uncontrollably." After a while, David calms down a bit. Off in the distance he hears a small indiscernible voice say, "pray." David lowers himself to the ground and begins to pray, "Father hear my cry and deliver me from the hands of my oppressors. I will not let fear overcome me. But I will trust you lord and know in my heart that you are lord over all. Your will be done. I am blessed to be your servant. Amen." This calms David even more, and he resigns himself to stay calm and be bold in the face of his enemies. After a while he nods off to sleep for almost an hour when the key to the cell door jangles and the door opens. It's the same soldier who brought him in earlier. "Get on your feet!" The guard escorts David to a room lit by candlelight. The same captain David met on his first encounter is sitting behind a table. David's satchel is on the table unopened. The guard brings David inside and pushes him down onto a bench opposite the captain. The captain instructs him to remove the leather-bound strap from the prisoner's wrists. Once free, Captain Aurelius tells the guard to return to his post and close the door behind him.

Captain Aurelius stands and begins to pace, "It will not go well with you to withhold any information from me. We have spent a great deal of time and resources tracking you down, and I am not ready to waste any more. Many people have suffered a great deal because of your actions. I would advise you to start with who you are, and how you escaped from my prison the other day. Any details you omit will only come back to cause you greater pain later. So, I advise you to come clean now."

David closes his eyes to regain his composure. Again, off in the distance and almost imperceptibly he hears the words, "trust in me" so David opens his eyes and says, "My name is David Campbell. I am from a faraway place you have never heard of, and I have been brought here by my master, Jesus of Nazareth." Aurelius stops at this last proclamation and stares at David. He has been hearing more and more about this Jesus and knows the Jewish leadership has been trying to get their grips on him to control him as well. As Jesus' popularity grows, the threat of civil unrest grows. The populace can only be controlled as long as the majority of the population fears retribution. David continues, "The other night, a woman came into the cell and told me to follow her. The cell door was open. She helped me up and we left the cell. Each door we came to was ajar. When we opened the door fully, there was no noise, not even a squeak from the rusty hinges. We exited the prison without raising any alarms or attracting any attention."

"That is simply not possible! You were barely alive from the eight lashes you received, and I saw your head wound myself. What happened to those injuries? How do you explain all the doors being unlocked?" Aurelius demands.

David knows the real answer, and he hesitates to say it. He takes a deep breath and continues, "There is no explanation other than to say my master, Jesus desired for me to escape. Miraculously, he arranged for the guards and prisoners to be asleep, the doors to be unlocked and just the two of us to be aware of our surroundings enough to walk out of here undetected and unharmed. It wasn't any one man who did this, it was a miracle done by God's Son. There is no other explanation. As for my injuries, you are right, they were so severe I could hardly walk. I needed assistance to make it out of the prison. When I met with Jesus a day later, he touched my hand, and immediately I felt his power course through my body. My wounds were healed instantly."

Aurelius walks around the table shaking his head with an angry look on his face. "Not possible. You lie!" He starts for his sword with one hand and gets it halfway out of the scabbard. He grabs David by the arm with his other hand. At that exact moment, an electric charge surges from David's arm through the captain. Sparks fly from his contact and Captain Aurelius convulses and falls backwards onto the floor. David doesn't know what has happened, and he jumps to his feet. He looks at his arm where Captain Aurelius touched him. There is nothing there. He watches Aurelius on the floor as he convulses and thrashes about almost like he is having a seizure. There is enough noise from the thrashing that a guard comes to the door and knocks, "Is everything all right in there, Captain?" David moves to the far corner of the room. He is afraid the guard will open the door and think he has done something to the captain of the guard. "Captain?" The guard asks again. He is wary of doing anything that will get him into trouble.

Suddenly, Aurelius awakens and looks up at David. David is afraid he will call for the other guard or worse, take out his anger directly with his sword still halfway out of its scabbard on his hip. Instead, Aurelius reaches up with his hand and asks David to help him to his feet. David hesitates at first to take his hand, but there is something familiar in the look of the captain's eyes. The guard starts to open the door, and Aurelius races to it pulling his sword completely out and holding it up to the neck of the guard trying to enter. "I'm sorry Captain, I heard noises and thought you had been overcome by the stranger." At this Aurelius holds the blade even tighter against his neck and draws a bit of blood. Aurelius replies, "The day I need you to protect me from the likes of him is the day I take my own life! Now get out and disturb me again only if you want to take his place!" The guard backs away holding his neck to stem the trickling flow of blood.

Captain Aurelius looks back at David and asks, "How long was I out and lying on the floor?" His demeanor has changed slightly. David replies, "Only about a minute or so, why? What just happened to you?"

"I'm not entirely sure. It felt like my entire life flashed before my eyes, and I have had what I can only say is a vision of my future. I lost all sense of time and awareness. If you would have told me I was laying there for three hours, I would have believed you. More importantly, I now understand everything you have been saying."

"What exactly does that mean?" David is still confused by the sudden change in his captor's attitude.

Aurelius is excited. He looks around to be sure he is secure and whispers, "I have met Jesus. Now, I am also a believer and even though this transformation admittedly has taken only a few minutes, it feels like I have been building up to the experience my whole life. I welcome it. A moment ago, I was the enemy who just wanted to keep a tight rein on the people primarily by hurting people. I have been given a new charge. It sounds strange because I look around and realize I never physically left this room. But I swear I have just spent the last several hours in his presence."

David nods, "Yeah, he has a way of doing that to people. It is hard to shake the feeling and realize you aren't in Kansas anymore." Aurelius just gives him a strange unknowing stare. David stops when he realizes the context of what he has just said, then continues, "It's a saying about a place where I am from... sorry, never mind. Please continue."

"He showed me everything I must do to help grow his ministry. How I will change the hearts and minds of many of my fellow Romans. I need to be patient and very careful in my approach. The change will take time, and there will be difficult times ahead. He was brutally honest with me about how dangerous a challenge it would be, but he promised a better life for me and my family. All of my previous knowledge and understanding about the afterlife was washed away. It was replaced with a view of heaven with him living eternally. I know this sounds crazy, but I felt love from him and compassion for the struggles ahead. It seems right that you are the first person I share my story with."

David is amazed, "That is an incredible testimony. I almost wish I could stay and witness it with you. Given your change of heart and purpose, what do you plan to do with me? I need to get back to Joshua's house, and I know this will also sound strange, but I need to climb onto his roof in order to return to my home."

"We will have to get you out of here without raising suspicion," Aurelius adds. He grabs the satchel off the table and walks over to David. Then he grabs his arm, pulls him over to the door and says, "Follow my lead no matter what you hear me say and do." He shouts through the door, "Guard, open the door!" This freaks David out, but he figures in for a penny in for a pound. The door opens and the guard from earlier pokes his head inside the room. He has a scarf wrapped around his neck to cover the cut from Aurelius' blade earlier. "Yes sir?"

Aurelius replies, "I'm taking the prisoner to the village. He has agreed to show me the location of his co-conspirators who helped him escape the other night. I want you to come with me and help with the arrest of the traitors." David's eyes go wider at the thought of the guard coming with them. He tries to adjust the plan, "I told you I would show only you." The captain looks at David and punches him in the stomach hard enough for David to double over coughing to catch his breath.

"I don't take orders from you," Aurelius states. "If you aren't willing to follow mine, we can just chain you up to the post, and give you more lashes until you pass out again! Or worse, end up like your previous cell mates!"

"No, I will take you as you say," David manages to speak. The guard smiles at the thought of David's suffering and of finding his conspirators. David is glad they haven't aroused his suspicion, but his stomach wished it could have been done without a punch to the gut.

The three head out of the prison back towards Joshua's house. When they get close to the house but still far enough away so the guard won't see the actual house, Captain Aurelius says, "post yourself here in case anyone makes a break and tries to circle back around."

"But sir, I want to assist in the capture," the guard replies. At this statement Aurelius gives a glare and says, "Disobey one more order, and you will find yourself in chains feeling the crack of my whip." The guard snaps to attention, "Yes sir! It won't happen again." Aurelius continues to glare at him, "See that it doesn't!"

The two of them round a corner and David indicates this is the location where he needs to climb on the roof. Aurelius sets himself to assist him. David pulls himself up and Aurelius then takes a handful of dirt and rubs it into his own face. He kneels down and pretends to be disoriented. He has to make the guard believe David distracted him by throwing dirt in his face and then escaping. Just as David gets on top of the house, Joshua comes out of the house, "What's going on up there?" He sees David and shouts, "You! What are you doing on top of my house again? Get down!" The guard hears the commotion and comes running to see Aurelius kneeling. He sees David on the roof. The guard runs and leaps onto the roof and scrambles to his feet to chase after David. When David gets to the patch in the roof, he closes his eyes, says a quick prayer and jumps down. The centurion lunges for him and grabs him by the collar of his robe. He leaps after David into the same hole in the roof holding onto his robe. Joshua watches the action on the roof and when both men disappear, he runs into the house to confront them. The centurion is lying in a heap holding onto on the robe, but David is nowhere to be found. The robe is empty. The centurion has twisted his ankle. Aurelius comes into the room wiping his face. "Where is he? Did you capture him?" He reaches down to give the centurion a hand up as he winces in pain putting weight on his sore ankle. Joshua looks up to see a large hole in his roof again.

"Where did he go?" He looks through the robe and looks around. The centurion points his finger at Joshua, "I don't see him. Where did he go? I fell through holding on to him! How is this possible?"

Joshua shakes his head, looks around at the guard, "I ran in just as both of you fell through my roof. He disappeared without a trace."

"How is that possible? I was right behind him," the guard yells.

Joshua shakes his head, "I swear to you. You are the only one who came down from the roof. I thought the other man fell before you, but he never appeared anywhere, and I don't see him now." Joshua is a bit more nervous now and wonders what will happen next. "I learned my lesson after the last time dealing with this man. I was the one who alerted the centurions that captured him only a few hours ago. I promise you, if he escaped again, I had nothing to do with it."

A few moments earlier, as David jumped onto the patch in the roof just ahead of the guard, instead of landing in a heap in front of Joshua, he kept falling in a swirling cavalcade of a blinding storm. It's the same thing he felt from the other day when he ended up in a heap at the floor of Joshua's home. This time however, as disorienting as this experience is, David has a sense of accomplishment and satisfaction. He hopes everything will turn out all right, and then instantly everything goes black.

CHAPTER 8

A FACE IN SAFETY

"Blessed is the one whose sin the Lord will never count against them." Romans 4:8 NIV

A woman's voice in the distance barely audible initially, grows in volume. After a moment, she can be heard more clearly. Candlelight appears. Everything comes into focus. Kathleen is bent over David trying to wake him up. Tim is hovering over him with Patty.

"Wake up David! David?" Kathleen continues to lightly shake him. "Oh, please David, wake up!"

David begins to stir and finally his eyes flutter and then open. He has trouble focusing at first, but then everything begins to clear up and David says, "What happened? Where am I?"

"You disappeared from the group, and it took us about forty-five minutes, but thank God we finally found you down here in this room. You must have fallen through that spot up there." Kathleen points up behind David's head. He turns and looks at the spot, and like a wave crashing on the shore all of his memory from the past two days is restored. It's almost too much to handle and David in a fit, tries to stand up. He winces in pain, staggers and sits back down with Kathleen's help. It's so real in David's mind and even though he is settling into the fact that he is back in his own time, it still feels like that centurion will come crashing through the roof any second and drag him back to the prison.

"Easy David," Tim says, "you have had a pretty nasty fall, and you were unconscious until now. We have called for an ambulance to come and get you. You may have a concussion from that nasty bump on your head, and your shoulder may be dislocated. Please just try to sit there and relax until help arrives. We don't want to take any chances with any kind of head or spinal injury."

David nods in agreement, "I think I'm okay, but I'll take your sound advice and just sit here a while longer." David is feeling a bit of Deja Vu with the same injuries, but glad to be back in his own time.

Patty wipes the tears from her face, steps closer and says, "Dad you really gave us a scare! First, we had no idea where you wandered off, and then when we found you down here unconscious. It really scared me. Mom must have been shaking you for a whole minute before you finally came around."

Kathleen asks, "What happened to you? Why did you leave the group?"

"Honestly it happened so fast. I had stopped to draw some flowers nearby and I remember spotting a woman waving at me, so I followed her." Kathleen looks quizzically at David, and David nods slightly telling Kathleen everything she needs to know that he had another encounter with his mystery woman again. David continues, "I followed her to a spot

115

above the hole there. She mysteriously disappeared but when I looked down, there was a light below me. I hopped down to check it out not realizing how far down it actually was. I hit hard and I remember crashing through from above. Did you say it took you forty-five minutes to find me?" Kathleen nods. "Wow, I have to say, it feels like it was a lot longer than that."

Tim tells him, "David, you missed most of today's tour, but because of your wandering, you appear to have stumbled upon the best find of the entire day! Not wishing any harm to you, I am glad you found this treasure trove. These pieces and furnishings here are fairly well preserved. They date back at least two thousand years. It appears to be a house and there are some amazing artifacts. The owner must have been a craftsman of some kind. There is a table with an elaborate etching of the Matterhorn. How a person in the time of Jesus would know what the Matterhorn looked like is hard to fathom. So, the tour got a lot more interesting because of your wandering. It appears to be a carpenter's shop. Some archaeologists are going to have a heyday going through everything you have uncovered. Frankly, they will be amazed that this chamber even exists and is so well preserved. Most of the other sites around here are covered in tons of dirt, and have to be carefully dug out while looking for anything of historical significance."

The ambulance arrives after a bit. The medics drop a long ladder down into the room followed by a stretcher where everyone is waiting. After assessing David's wounds, they give him a small dosage of pain medication to take the edge off. The 1st medic says in heavily accented English, "We cannot give you anything too strong because you have a concussion injury. We cannot risk you falling asleep." David nods his approval.

They wrap his head wound. The dislocated arm is immobilized with a sling and tie down that goes around his waist. This causes David to experience a new wave of pain that makes him nauseous. The medic sees the result of tightening the strap and says, "I'm afraid you may also have a cracked rib or two as well. We won't know the full extent of the damage until you get to the hospital and have x-rays taken." With Tim and Kathleen's assistance, they lift David onto the stretcher. David's shoulder screams out in pain with every movement. He holds it back as much as possible. As they lift David almost vertically through the ceiling, he looks back down at the room and feels a touch of sadness at leaving. David is glad to be back home safe and reunited with his family. It is all so hard to believe. The experience is still fresh in his mind. But he cannot help thinking about the fate of his recent friends. He wonders about Captain Aurelius, Mary and the disciples. It still feels like the episode is still happening. The experience has been incredible.

The stretcher ride back to the ambulance is bumpy, but now the medication has kicked in and the pain is dulled slightly. Kathleen stays right by his side the entire time, and rides next to David in the ambulance. She holds onto his good hand and converses with him to keep him alert. After a bit, David is able to relax and he drifts into a half awake half dreaming state of awareness.

At the hospital, the doctor looks over the x-rays and confirms his shoulder is dislocated and it will be very painful to put it back in place. The doctor grabs an arm and the bad shoulder and asks the nurse to hold his other side. He asks

David if he is ready, and David nods. The doctor holds David's arm and shoulder and gives a quick push. It hurts like hell. It is about the same amount of pain as the last time, but he much preferred Dr. Solomon's approach with not giving him any prior notice before resetting the shoulder. However, David thinks the pain meds are a definite improvement over the old days. The doctor bandages up his head, puts his arm in a sling, and prescribes some antibiotics to prevent further infection. Finally, he is released and they make their way back to the King David Hotel. Once in the room, David tells Kathleen he has some additional information he wants to share with her about his experience. David remembers Jesus' warning about sharing his true experience with people, and he decides he would not share the full story with Patty, at least for now. But Kathleen needs to know because she already knows a part of the story about the mystery woman from his dreams. It weighs on David about the potential consequences of telling Kathleen about his experience because of Jesus' warning. In the end he wasn't forbidden from telling, just warned to be very selective.

"You are going to want to be sitting down to hear the whole story of what happened to me. There is way more to it than the version I gave back at the excavation site." Kathleen sits down on the couch opposite of David. She already knows the mystery woman was involved from earlier. David begins recanting his entire saga. He tells her how he ended up in that same room except two thousand years earlier. He was hurt then too, but was bandaged and fixed up by the local doctor. Kathleen is studying David intensely while hearing the story unfold. She wants to believe him, but it is just too fantastic. It has to have been a dream, albeit an elaborate one caused by the severe blow to his head. When David gets to the part of the lashings by the centurion guard, he stands up and takes off his shirt and turns to reveal his back to Kathleen. She is mortified at the sight of the scars left by the centurion's whip. She asks, "but if you just got these, how on earth are they already healed and scarred over?" David replies, "I'm getting to that part, and if you are amazed so far, just wait!"

"More like stunned," Kathleen retorts.

Up until then, she believes David has lived through an intricate and complex dream. She asks about the Matterhorn carving found at the site, and David tells her that he had given Joshua his drawing from the sketchpad. He must have liked it and carved it into one or more of his carpentry works. He tells her about being tossed into prison after his beating. How he feared for his life and met other men of the time trapped in the prison as well. Next, he tells about his meeting Mary, his mystery woman, and their miraculous escape from the prison. When he starts describing his experience with the disciples, David opens up his sketchpad and introduces Kathleen to Mary, James, Matthew and Judas. She begins to weep. "Oh David, this is incredible. It seems so impossible and yet I know in my heart and in my head it must be true. I feel so honored and blessed."

"I know, it's wonderful, but I really saved the best for last." David then describes his meeting Jesus. I was sitting and Jesus reached for me. As he lifted me up, I felt a surge of energy flow through my body. In that instance, all my wounds were healed. He then tells her all the things Jesus had spelled out for him. How Jesus had restored his faith and more than that, he had re-energized his passion for gospel ministry. Next, he shows her the picture of Jesus, and Kathleen starts to smile at the thought of Jesus laughing. "Oh my, David," she says, "is this really him?"

"Yes, you know me, I draw as close to real as I possibly can. His insight into my life and struggles was profound. And before you ask, yes, he really was laughing and that was the moment in time I chose to capture. It seemed perfectly timed. Here was this man and his disciples living in such a rugged and humble way, and yet they were happy to be doing their ministry. Jesus had not revealed the full aspect of his being to them as yet, but the magnitude of the change they were making for the entire world was so palpable to me because I knew where he was taking them in the long run."

Kathleen asks, "What instrumental advice did he give you to change your heart and restore your faith? As if meeting him in person wouldn't have been enough for anyone!"

"You're right," David continued. "Just meeting Jesus was a big part of my restoration. He told me I was specifically chosen by God for this rare encounter. He also told me to keep preaching because people hearing the word of God is the most important thing. He said bringing the light to a single person pleases his father. My time with him was intimate and life altering. But at the same time, people who hear the word of God and believe without seeing him first hand will be blessed beyond measure."

Kathleen asks, "Are you going to tell Bill about your extraordinary experience when you get back home? I know he will be pleased about your renewed vigor about teaching and continuing your mission together."

"I don't think so," David replies. "I was expressly warned by Jesus against telling people my story because it would be a giant leap to believe it, and could cause more harm than good. I'm sure Bill will be satisfied that my pastor's burnout has been extinguished! I actually considered telling Patty the full story, but chose not to because I didn't want to have to swear her to secrecy, and put any additional undo pressure on her. Teenagers have enough problems all on their own!"

"That is interesting. I guess it makes sense why. Honestly, even I was skeptical at the beginning of your story until you took your shirt off. I'm really glad you decided to share this with me. So, is that when you awoke in the room, or is there more story to tell?" Kathleen asked.

"No, there's more," David replied. "In order to complete my journey, I had to travel back to Joshua's house, the place where you found me, and literally climb back on the roof to jump back through the same hole. Only then would I be restored to my time. There were still moments when I thought I would be found out and never make it back home to you. I nearly panicked at the thought, but I found peace in Jesus' words which were simple but powerful, 'Trust in my Father with all of your mind, body and soul.' Believe it or not, I found myself back in the same prison having been re-captured just as I got back to Joshua's house."

Kathleen's eyes grow wild, "Oh my goodness! You were back in prison? That had to be scary."

David continues, "I really thought to myself, this is the end, but then I remembered Jesus' words and was able to truly relax and be at peace with any outcome. As it turns out, a Roman Captain named Aurelius was in control of my fate at this point. Quite unexpectedly, he experienced his own revelation about God in a pretty profound way as well. As a result of his own encounter, he assisted in my escape from prison and got me back to Joshua's house. Still, I was spotted and chased on the roof by the same Roman guard who captured me before. Jumping through the hole in Joshua's roof is the last thing I remember before waking up with all of you around me. By the way, that was the second time dislocating my shoulder in as many days!"

Kathleen and David sit there for a while silent. David takes a moment to pray with his wife. Finally, they hear a knock at their bedroom door. "Hey!" Patty shouts from the other side, "can I come in? I want to see how dad is doing!"

"Sure, kiddo, come on in!" David answers. Patty opens the door and bounces in. She gives both parents a kiss on the head, and sits down next to her dad. "How are you feeling Dad?" Patty asks.

"I feel great! And I can't wait to continue our travels. We still have a whole week to explore and experience this wonderful land," David says.

Kathleen admonishes him slightly, "Okay, but you won't be out of our sight for one minute unless it's to go to the bathroom. Do you hear me?"

David nods, "Aye-aye, captain!"

For the next week, the trio travel around Israel seeing as many sights as they can take in. David has a new appreciation for the places he visits. He keeps looking over his shoulder and other directions for his mystery lady, but she never reappears. A couple of times Kathleen asks him if he is seeing anything out of the ordinary, and tells her no. David remains on a mental high for rest of the trip. His wounds are healing up nicely. The dislocated shoulder still aches when he makes certain movements. It will never be the same as he gets older, but he resolves to think of what he went through every time he winces in pain. He promises himself he will focus on Jesus. He also knows there will still be tough times ahead, but right now, in this moment he is still feeling overjoyed and blessed by his experience. He is grateful to Kathleen for her participation and affirmation. It's going to be hard to top this vacation.

CHAPTER 9

A FACE BACK HOME

"The people walking in darkness have seen a great light."
Isaiah 9:2 NIV

The flight back to the United States from Israel is long and without incident. The three of them sleep a good portion of the trip home. After clearing customs in Los Angeles, it hits David hard knowing the magic of the vacation is truly over. It is a bit of a let down because he has been so emotionally charged for the entire trip. Now, the realization of getting back to reality sets in on him. They take a few days relaxing at home to get over the jet lag and to recover from the trip. Patty still has a couple weeks of summer vacation left, so she spends the days catching up with her friends. Kathleen plans to meet up with a few of her girlfriends to share her experiences from the vacation of a lifetime. On her way out the door David gives her a knowing glance about the limits of her sharing. Kathleen responds in kind but nods her understanding. David spends a fair amount of time working on his sermon for this weekend. He is excited and totally ready to be back in the pulpit. He has also reached out to Bill via text, telling him the trip was fantastic, and he is ready to take on new challenges. David can practically feel the excitement in Bill's text response asking to meet with David at the church at his earliest convenience. They set their meeting for Friday.

When Friday morning arrives, David heads to the church with his satchel in hand. He gets to church a bit early because he wants to get some things organized in his office before he meets with Bill. David takes the drawings of the disciples and Jesus and arranges them out on his desk. He spent the last couple days adding watercolors to the drawings trying to draw from his memory the particular nuances of color in the skin, hair and the surrounding foliage. The added affect of the colors to the drawings has eerily made them come to life for David. He is lost in thought staring at the drawings when he looks up and realizes Bill is standing in his doorway waiting for David to look up.

"Bill!" David finally acknowledges, "it's so good to see you! Come in!" David stands and comes around his desk to warmly greet Bill with a hug.

"I was standing there for a moment just admiring you, admiring your drawings," Bill says.

David releases Bill and looks back at them. He moves back to sit and motions for Bill to have a seat as well. "Yes," David continues, "I'm using these in my sermon this weekend, but I wanted them out for the continuation of our discussion from our previous meeting where I called you out. First of all, I want to apologize for how I behaved to you. It was unkind and definitely not a way to treat my dearest and most trusted longtime friend. I also wanted to thank you for giving me the time to work out some of my issues. I was in a difficult mindset."

Bill is intrigued, and says, "Good! That meeting didn't end well, so I'm glad this is a continuation to hopefully end on a better note! Haha!"

"Indeed!" David chuckles too. "To set your mind at ease, I'm ready to fully re-engage in my lead pastor role." Bill nods and breathes a sigh of relief. "But," David continues, "I have a couple conditions I want to run by you to make sure you and I have the same goals in mind for the outreach portion of our ministry." Bill nods in agreement and David continues to speak, "I have a passion for the poor and disenfranchised in our region that has only grown over the past few months. I want to start a new ministry to help these people and call it 'Feed-Clothe-Shelter-Employ' which would go way above and beyond what our church has done in the past to support the people who are suffering and needing a helping hand to restore their lives. I want us to gather food, clothing, health care items, basic commodities needed to survive, and provide a sanctuary for people without a home to come and find rest within these walls. I know drug use amongst many of these people will make this a difficult task especially for the final piece, finding them employment. The truth is there are many poor people nearby and practically in our own neighborhoods who desperately need our help. It's high time we give it to them. I'm a realist and know that we cannot solve the problem for all the people, but I want to do as much as we can. And, if we take a strong enough leadership role in this undertaking, other churches will follow our lead on this."

Bill pauses a moment to consider what David is asking. "But David," Bill replies, "ministries like this require serious funding and almost more importantly, leaders to make it happen, to inspire people to volunteer and keep it alive for the long haul. I'm in total agreement and honestly after hearing the passion in your voice, excited by the prospect. My inner organizer person is screaming to approach something like this with extreme caution. First of all, we have to think of someone to head this undertaking."

"Exactly," David shakes his head emphatically. "I wanted to clear it with you first, but I'm excited by the prospect, and feel like this is real kingdom work to be done. I even hope the state government will take notice and potentially provide additional funding along the way. I know we have the right congregation to get behind this ministry, and I also know we will find the right leaders because God will show up and show us the way through prayer. In the long run, the hard work and glitches along the way will lead to a huge blessing upon all of us for doing something extraordinary in the lives of these families."

Bill replies, "okay, it sounds like an exciting ministry, and I agree we should move forward, but first, I'm curious about the drawings on your desk! They look awesome, but are they part of this discussion above and beyond your sermon prep?"

A broad grin forms on David. He definitely won't tell Bill his full experience, but he did discuss a strategy with Kathleen of telling him certain aspects of his journey without disclosing the true full nature. David says, "I'm glad you noticed and yes, they are part of this discussion because they have played a big part in my journey and transformation these past few weeks. In my travels through the Holyland, and as I learned about the historical significance of each site, I became fascinated with, almost consumed with the idea of being there as the actual events unfolded over two thousand years ago. I tried to imagine what it would have been like to travel alongside the disciples of Jesus. It must have been a very difficult and oppressive time trying to do ministry, but also very rewarding. I meditated deeply and prayed for guidance in our ministry. God met me and transported me in those times of meditation. These drawings are the result. They represent a few of the men and women who travelled with our lord and who learned and then taught what it is like to be a disciple of Jesus. Jesus is the focus of course, but it's his disciples like you and I and these people in the picture who help people understand and spread the gospel. We need to continue to reach as many people as we can, and help the people who already come to grow into more authentic Christians. To be disciples in their own rights and bring God's kingdom into their lives outside of these walls." David raises his arms and points to the sanctuary for emphasis.

Bill reaches down and picks up the second drawing and says, "That is powerful, and a beautiful vision my friend. I'm totally on board. Which disciple is this?"

David chuckles and says, "You'll have to see my sermon to learn the full identity of this person, but I can tell you he is the first disciple."

"Well, he's laughing, which is surprising," Bill continues, "so, it couldn't have been all bad, at least in your mind to have drawn him this way."

David takes a deep breath remembering the moment captured in the picture, "no, not all bad at all."

The next day, David is standing in the pulpit delivering his first sermon since returning. David looks up from the pulpit, "I want to thank all of you for allowing me the time off to take a sabbatical. Also, a special thank you from Kathleen and Patty. We spent the time as most of you know in the Holyland, and it was for me the most profound experience I will ever have in my life. And I truly have all of you to thank for this gift. I took a lot of the time drawing my experiences while we were there which I'm displaying up on the screens behind me. These first couple pictures are of disciples. As you might have guessed from how they are dressed, this is my rendition of disciples from Jesus' time. As I would meditate on a particular historical site, I felt so immersed in the culture that I lost myself in what it means to be one of his disciples." David flips through the slides of the disciples and discusses each one individually. Finally he stops on the one of Jesus. "This is my second portrayal of Jesus. Only this time I have drawn him through a different lens. The last time I showed him as sad because of our sin. But I really want to emphasize how happy he is when one of us believes. So, I show him laughing because I believe we please the Lord to the point of absolute enjoyment when we become a true believer in the grace and goodness of His gospel." David then shows individual pictures of congregation members on the screens and announces each one, "Natasha, disciple. Lauren, disciple. Curtis, disciple. Jeff, disciple. Marcus, disciple. Each one of these people and many many more in this room make Jesus laugh every day when you bring the good news to the world." David puts Jesus' picture back up on the screens. "When you go to work, or go out to dinner, or simply walk down the street, always reflect on the people around you what it means to be a disciple of Jesus."

The sermon has ended and David is in the lobby greeting members of the congregation. Bill introduces David to Brittany and Dan Landing who takes them off to the side to discuss their involvement in the new Feed-Clothe-Shelter-Employ ministry. Bill is immediately impressed at their exuberance and ideas for the ministry. They both have a lot of experience in ministry and specifically working with the poor from their previous church. They are especially excited in the prospect of this new ministry because it represents a significant change to how people reach out to help the poor.

After a while, David excuses himself to let them continue their discussions. He sees Marcus amongst the crowd and approaches him. Marcus complements him on his sermon and tells him the pictures he showed were very inspirational. "I almost feel like I was there with Jesus and his disciples. Next, he thanks David for reaching out regarding his job situation. He tells him that he has received a very generous offer with a company. David smiles and congratulates him. Gradually, the lobby empties, and David is able to pack up his satchel and head for home.

Later that night, after everyone has gone to bed, David quietly walks into Patty's room. He glances down at his sleeping daughter, then walks over to his drawing of Patty mounted on the wall. David reaches into his pocket, pulls out a pencil and signs his picture.

David C. Campbell

The End

ABOUT THE AUTHOR

Jeff McKenzie is a husband, father and grandfather with aspirations of writing for many years to come. This story has been inside his mind for many years. Some of the story about David's journey in this novel come from Jeff's direct experiences with his faith. Writing and storytelling, as difficult as they can be, provide an outlet and a chance to be alone with God.

Thank you Ken, Becky, Sherman, Rita, Ron, Kathleen, Bob and my wife Carolyn for all your support and help in bringing this book to life! Enjoy!

Made in the USA
Las Vegas, NV
20 February 2021